HURTING

LISA NORBY

SCHOLASTIC INC.
New York Toronto London Auckland Sydney

ISBN 0-590-33929-X

Copyright © 1986 by Lisa Norby. All rights reserved. Published by Scholastic Inc.

12 11 10 9 8 7 6 5 4 3 2 ˆ   6 7 8 9/8 0 1/9

Printed in the U.S.A.   01

CHEERLEADERS

HURTING

CHEERLEADERS

Trying Out

Getting Even

Rumors

Feuding

All the Way

Splitting

Flirting

Forgetting

Playing Games

Betrayed

Cheating

Staying Together

Hurting

Living It Up

"What's the matter with you⸻ trust Walt?" Angie Poletti aske⸻

"Of course I trust him."⸻ studied her image in the f⸻ girls' locker room. The ⸻ appeared in her boy⸻ by the pleated skirt⸻ Tarenton High c⸻ at times, more ⸻ than a junior ⸻ than she seer⸻ her determi⸻

It was ⸻ away. Big, ⸻ eyebrows ti⸻ those eyes ⸻ feelings. A ⸻ ing was ur⸻

isn't a question of trust," Olivia tried to
to Angie. "Walt's really solid. I know that.
's only human, too, and I keep thinking
alone at tonight's pool party surrounded
ls with gorgeous figures in their little
. And in the meantime, I'll be stuck with
rents."

ia had been shanghaied by her folks into
ng a family wedding out of state over the
d. The wedding itself wouldn't be so bad,
she hadn't seen the cousin who was get-
arried since they were in grade school.
ing stuck in the car with her mother for
g drive both ways was going to be a kind
torture. "Mom means well," she thought
ut sometimes she nearly nags me to

bit. "I can sympathize with
e said. "My mother can be
st she never fusses over
crazy to be nervous
n, lighten up!"
to the mirror. She
a shake, all the
her hair back
. ." she said

gie laughed.
end?"
pted by the
of the half-
ed out onto

the court and joined the rest of the cheering squad.

Mary Ellen Kirkwood, the squad captain, had taken no break at all. She gave the latecomers a quick glance of disapproval before lifting the megaphone to her lips to launch into another cheer:

"Our team is RED HOT!
Their team is ALL SHOT!"

Walt Manners, one of the squad's two male members, suddenly appeared on the court dressed in a slightly seedy fake-fur suit and papier-mâché head as Tarenton's mascot, the wolf. Walt responded to the "Red Hot" cheer by producing a fake torch with crimson crepe paper "flames." First, he twirled the torch like a baton. Then, with a snap of his wrist he unfolded the crepe-paper streamers to their full length and used them as a jump rope.

Angie led the pep section in showing its appreciation with a rhythmic clapping. Walt always made his antics look easy and spontaneous. Having watched Walt work out his tricks during practice, she knew that this was all an illusion. That wolf suit was so bulky that just running around in it, much less skipping rope, took tremendous coordination. Not to mention the problem of throwing and catching a baton while wearing that awkward wolf's head.

Inspired by Walt's efforts, Angie put some

3

extra oomph into her cheers. The Tarenton five were already leading the Chateaugay Cheetahs by eighteen points, and since the game didn't even count toward the conference standings, the atmosphere in the gym was hardly reeking of suspense.

Angie remembered what Coach Engborg had told them earlier in the week: It's easy to get a crowd going during the big games; the real test of a cheerleading squad is keeping the energy level high during the games that might otherwise be yawners.

Actually, Angie needed this advice less than any other member of the squad. She had a naturally outgoing personality, and she never felt so good, so completely alive, as when she was out on the court, doing her cheering routines in front of a fired-up crowd.

That was the best part of being a cheerleader, Angie often thought. Caught up in the excitement of cheering, the members of the squad forgot their petty personal problems. The squad became a unit — a bundle of energy and high spirits capable of making an entire crowd feel good.

Elated by the thought, Angie motioned for Pres Tilford, the second male cheerleader, to give her a boost up onto his shoulders. Pres held her aloft for almost a whole minute so that she could direct her cheers to the kids in the upper rows of the bleachers.

When she had leaped back down to the court, Pres couldn't resist giving Angie a good-natured

4

nudge in the ribs. Angie was bouncy and cute, but she was no sylph. "Pretty soon we're going to have to change places on that trick," he joked.

Angie was a good sport. Of all the girls on the squad, she was the one you could count on to take a bit of harmless teasing in the right spirit.

Tall, blond, and confident of his power to make female hearts beat faster, Pres never dreamed that with his humorous remark he had just deflated Angie's good mood.

Having to be ferried to the after-game pool party, in the backseat of her brother Andrew's VW, did nothing to restore Angie's good cheer.

Andrew, a junior, was always generous about seeing that Angie had transportation, even when he had a date. Tonight, however, Andrew's attention was completely focused on Kerry Elliot, the little curly-haired girl from the sophomore class who had recently started seeing him again after her breakup with Pres. Stuffed into the car's tiny backseat, Angie felt like an overgrown kid. Sulky, uncomfortable, and completely superfluous.

This, she told herself, was not how the dream of being a senior cheerleader was supposed to work out.

A senior girl who made cheerleader was supposed to be overwhelmed with dates. She ought to be so popular that her final year in high school would be like a triumphal parade, taking her from one peak of popularity to the next.

True, the other members of the Tarenton High

squad had their problems, Angie reflected. But at least they weren't so far from fulfilling the dream that they had to go to parties with their little brothers!

Nancy Goldstein, Angie thought, came the closest of any girl on the squad to living up to the ideal image. Nancy was blessed by fate with everything a girl could wish for: A perfect figure, with a tiny waist and a generous chest measurement. Parents wealthy enough to keep her supplied with a constant stream of designer outfits. The brains to keep a straight "A" average while still enjoying a full schedule of activities and parties. Nancy had her pick of boyfriends, too.

At the moment she was going out with sexy Ben Adamson, a varsity basketball player and recent transfer student whose tough-guy exterior had turned out to house a sensitive nature. But the list of Nancy's rejects was enough to make almost any other girl in school green with envy. Josh Breitman, to name one, was a real dreamboat. Who but Nancy would have had the nerve to reject a guy like Josh because she considered him dull, of all things!

Then there was Mary Ellen Kirkwood, the squad captain and a tall, willowy blonde. Mary Ellen couldn't afford the kind of expensive clothes that Nancy sported. But then again, she didn't need them. Angie sometimes wondered what it would be like to know that you could make a career, even earn big money, just on the strength of your looks. That was how Mary Ellen saw her future, and she was probably right. Mary Ellen had the right looks and the single-minded discipline to make it as a big-time model, or even as an actress.

What's more, if she ever changed her mind, Mary Ellen had brawny, happy-go-lucky Patrick Henley just waiting in the wings to marry her. Pres liked to say that Mary Ellen treated Patrick like a yo-yo, pulling the string in accordance with her whim at the moment. But nothing she did ever seemed to discourage Patrick's fixation on her.

Finally, continuing her countdown of the other girls on the squad, Angie got around to thinking about Olivia Evans. Olivia wasn't beautiful or especially smart. She wasn't about to win any personality contests, either. Not the way she acted: aloof and withdrawn one minute, and too nakedly emotional the next. But Olivia, of all people, had come the closest to finding true love of any of the girls.

Angie had known Walt Manners most of her life without ever feeling the slightest spark of sexual attraction to him. She knew Walt well enough, though, to realize that he was a great guy. Able to play the class clown and natural center of attention, but still be warm and caring about his friends.

Short and stocky, with a moon-shaped face, Walt had never been considered good-looking. Still, he was in top physical condition as a gymnast and a dancer, and it had occurred to Angie more than once that Walt was the type of guy who would probably keep on getting more attractive as he aged.

Olivia didn't know how lucky she was!

Thinking back to their conversation in the locker room at halftime, Angie sighed with exasperation. Imagine giving in to self-pity just because you had to be separated from your boyfriend for one little weekend!

No one thinks to worry about my feelings, Angie thought miserably. And I've really had the hard luck in the romance department.

For most of the year, she had gone to parties alone because her boyfriend Marc Filanno was away at college — only to get a "Dear Jane" letter breaking off the relationship as a reward for all her loyalty.

Then she'd swallowed her pride and started going out with Arne Peterson, the class brain. That, too, had ended with rejection, because Arne just didn't know what to make of a girl friend who considered cheerleading practice more important than going to classical concerts or gazing at the stars through a telescope. She and Arne had probably been a mismatch from the beginning, but it was no fun thinking that a guy you liked has stopped asking you out because you don't meet his standards in the I.Q. department.

Angie, Andrew, and Kerry were among the first to arrive at the Y.

Kerry took one look at the new olympic-sized pool, which was being inaugurated at tonight's party, and gave a breathy whistle of appreciation.

Unlike the old, rundown facility it replaced, this pool was big enough for serious swimming. The water, reflecting the colors of the blue and white tiled floor, sparkled invitingly. And the whole setup was enclosed in a new wood-paneled building with a high, vaulted roof and four skylights that revealed patches of starry sky overhead.

A banner along one wall of the enclosure said: WELCOME UNITED FUND VOLUNTEERS. The entire basketball team and cheerleading squad had been included in that lucky group because they had raised so much money for the fund at their student-faculty game. Judging by the amount of food weighing down the long tables under the banner, however, it looked as if they were going to be just part of a very large crowd.

"For once I'm glad to be early to a party," Angie said. "Let's change in a hurry and have a good swim before this place gets too packed."

Angie took her own advice and managed to get in a good ten-lap workout, alternating freestyle and backstroke. By the time she finished, some other kids from school had arrived. Not wanting to be caught doing anything seriously athletic, especially when she was supposed to be partying, she climbed out of the water and ran off to the locker room to give her sopping wet hair a quick drying.

When she came back out into the pool area again, she saw that the party was shaping up pretty much as she had imagined it. Nancy Goldstein, sleek in a hot-pink bikini and three gold neck chains, was standing conspicuously under the welcome banner, engaged in what looked like a very intimate conversation with Ben.

Patrick Henley was doing a jackknife off the springboard, literally twisting himself into knots in an attempt to impress Mary Ellen, who, naturally, was standing off in a corner pretending not to notice.

As for Pres, he had wasted no time zeroing in on the most beautiful nonstudent in the room. Wearing a confident smile and carrying two cold cans of soda, he was making a beeline for a tall brunette who happened to be sitting alone on a deck chair near the shallow end of the pool. She doesn't know it, Angie thought, but she's about to become the latest of Pres's glamorous "older woman" conquests. Though, in fairness, this particular brunette didn't look all that old.

Angie quickly scanned the room, hoping against hope to find the brunette's male counterpart — an exciting stranger who would sweep her off her feet. A quick glance told her that the only single male in the room who wasn't a student from Tarenton High was paunchy Mr. Marburg, a middle-aged teacher who was too earnestly boring to inspire even a passing fantasy.

Well, you can't win them all, Angie told herself. In fact, when it came to meeting boys at parties, she hadn't even been getting on the scoreboard lately.

Shrugging off the thought, she headed across the room to check out the refreshment table and have a comforting chat with Kerry.

CHAPTER

Angie was right about one thing: Pres had noticed the brunette stranger almost immediately and had decided that her presence was a challenge he could not afford to pass up.

Grabbing two cans of ice-cold sodas from the bin by the refreshment table, he made a beeline in the brunette's direction and settled into the reclining chair next to hers.

Close up, he noticed that the girl was wearing an obviously much-washed safari shirt over a simple black suit, no jewelry, and very little make-up. Pres liked the fashion-conscious types, and normally he wouldn't have given a second thought to any girl so underdressed, even at a pool party. This girl was clearly going to be an exception.

Long-legged and slim, she had an elegant figure and fine, absolutely straight black hair that fell nearly to her waist. And there was an aura of confidence about the way she was sitting, totally unconcerned about being alone at a party full of strangers. This was one girl who didn't need to dress up to get attention. In fact, she looked like a girl who needed no one and nothing at all — which only made Pres more determined to get a response.

"I thought you looked as if you could use a cold drink," he began, holding out the two cans he held for the girl's inspection. "Diet or regular? Take your choice."

"Why, isn't that sweet of ya'll?" The girl spoke with a lilting southern accent that turned what should have been a statement into a question. As if she were asking herself whether to be pleased by the gesture or not.

After the accent, Pres got a second happy surprise when the girl turned to face him. She had the most amazing eyes he'd ever seen, a deep, rich amethyst in color enriched by tiny flecks of gold. From a distance, the girl had looked classy and attractive but hardly stunning — not in the class of a real beauty like Mary Ellen Kirkwood. For once, Pres had to admit, his ability to size-up girls at a glance had failed him — this one he had underestimated by a mile.

The girl took the diet soda from Pres's hand, and he watched her take a sip, relieved to get rid of it before his rising temperature warmed the ice-cold drink to the boiling point.

Apparently, the girl was used to having her first glance stun men into admiring silence. "I'm Claudia Randall," she said.

13

"That's a lovely name."

Claudia waited for Pres to go on, then prompted him. "And you are. . . ?"

"Me?" Pres asked stupidly. "Oh, right. I'm Pres Tilford. Preston Tilford III, actually."

Pres's full name never failed to get a reaction, even from people new to Tarenton. This time, he was not disappointed.

"Isn't that interestin'," Claudia drawled. "As in the Tilfords who own Tarenton Fabricators."

A look of polite embarrassment flickered across her face. "I'm sorry. You must get terribly bored with that reaction to your name. I know it always drives me practically out of my mind when people are only interested in talking about my family. I know just how annoying that can be."

"You do?" Pres was intrigued. In his whole life, he'd never met anyone his age who had a clue as to what it would be like. That was the problem with being the only son of the richest, most powerful family in town. Everyone saw the advantages of being who you were. No one saw the drawbacks. And you could hardly complain about them very much without starting to sound spoiled and ungrateful, even to yourself.

"Up north here, being a Randall doesn't count for anything," Claudia explained. "But back where I'm from, it's like being a Tilford."

"Where *are* you from?" Pres asked, truly fascinated.

"Oh, just a little bitty town in Virginia," Claudia said. "No bigger than Tarenton."

"And your father's in business there?"

Claudia giggled as if Pres had just accused her father of something vaguely embarrassing.

"Not exactly. It's just that a few years ago Daddy decided to sell off some land that had been in the family for ages. The developer decided to call the houses he built there Randall Estates. After our plantation, y'know. The name kind of caught on after that, and now there's a Randall Mall, a Randall Heights Country Club, even a Randall Village National Bank.

"Of course," Claudia added, "my family doesn't own all of that. We're just ordinary folks, really."

"Oh, sure."

Pres had a fairly good idea that there was nothing ordinary about the Randalls. He could understand, though, Claudia's temptation to do a little bragging about her family even while she was telling him how boring it was to be singled out. That was part of the typical rich-kid complex — along with wearing good but well-worn clothes when you could well afford to buy new ones. There was a kind of reverse snobbery involved, he supposed. It was funny, though, that he'd always been attracted to girls who dressed up, even though he himself usually wore the most casual clothes he could get away with. Up until now.

"Tell me what it's like to be Pres Tilford III," Claudia invited him. "You may be a Yankee, but my guess is you're a little bit of a rebel, too."

Before he knew it, Pres was telling Claudia his

15

entire life story. He told her about how his family lived in the fanciest house out on Cedar Point, which was lucky because the house was big enough for them to avoid talking to each other for days at a time. He talked about how disappointed his father was that he, Pres, didn't want to attend Princeton. And about how his Dad really hated the fact that he'd passed up varsity sports to go out for cheerleading.

"I guess I only wanted to be a cheerleader in the first place because it seemed like the only thing I hadn't tried yet that would really annoy the hell out of my father," Pres confessed. "The funny thing is, I've stuck with it longer than almost anything I've ever done. Usually I start off with a lot of enthusiasm and then lose interest."

Claudia laughed. "Well, I certainly hope you're not going to lose interest in me that fast," she said.

Pres had played the cool, unflappable role long enough to know not to say anything that would commit him too quickly. But a little voice inside him answered the question with a hoot. Not this time, it exclaimed. Not when you've just found the first girl you could talk to without having to be constantly trying to explain what being Pres Tilford is all about!

Patrick, meanwhile, was striking out in his bid for Mary Ellen's attention. After fifteen or so daring dives, even he could see that a change of tactics was in order.

Never subtle, Patrick waited until Mary Ellen ventured into the water. Then he pursued her the length of the pool, using an energetic butterfly stroke that sent spouts of water splashing toward the ceiling and nearly drowned several nearby swimmers.

Mary Ellen watched his approach with mixed feelings, touched yet embarrassed at the same time. "Do you have to make such a spectacle of yourself?" she hissed when Patrick had reached her side.

He grinned. "Not *myself*. *Ourselves*. Everyone's staring at you, too, Mary Ellen."

"Maybe. But I'm not the one who's playing the fool," she protested.

"I can fix that," Patrick said with an inspired grin.

Grabbing Mary Ellen by the waist, Patrick hoisted her into the air and held her overhead, balanced on the palms of his powerful, work-hardened hands.

"Let me down," she shrieked. "Stop it!"

Sure enough, the maneuver had attracted amused grins and laughter from half the people at the party.

Mary Ellen tried hard to concentrate on her indignation, ignoring the weak, fluttery feeling in the pit of her stomach that always started up whenever Patrick touched her. "Get lost!" she ordered him. "Pronto."

Patrick ignored her. "Want to make a bet?" he suggested.

"No."

"How can you say no before you've even heard the terms?" he chided her.

"Easy. Because you have nothing I want," Mary Ellen lied.

"How about this, then? I'll bet you I can do a somersault off the high board. Starting from a handstand, yet. If I can't, I promise to stay out of your hair for a whole week. You won't even know I'm alive. Doesn't that sound tempting?"

"Patrick you are so impossible."

But Mary Ellen was considering the offer. "And what happens if you win?" she asked warily.

"If I win, then you go out on a date with me within the week."

Patrick looked even more pleased with himself than usual. "Some terms, aren't they? I make a terrific consolation prize. Just wait and see."

Mary Ellen studied the three-meter diving board with interest. Patrick was not a bad diver, but she was pretty sure he'd never even gone off a board that high until tonight.

"Okay," she agreed, "if you want to risk your life trying some hot dog dive, don't let me stop you. But remember, you've got to do it right or you lose."

"Fair's fair," Patrick said. He headed back for the deep end of the pool, milling his arms wildly in an even more exaggerated butterfly stroke.

It wasn't until he'd climbed up the ladder of the three-meter board that he began to consider whether there were some things not worth trying, even for love. The water, shimmering under the end of the board, looked awfully far away. And Mary Ellen had guessed right. He'd never tried to do a dive from a handstand in his entire life.

Nancy Goldstein looked up from her argument with Ben just in time to see Patrick balanced precariously in a handstand on the very edge of the high board.

"Oh, no!" she shrieked automatically.

Her voice was louder than she'd meant it to be, and it echoed off the far wall of the room. Everyone else had gone suddenly silent.

With a strangled grunt, Patrick launched himself into the air and into a somersault, his head barely clearing the end of the board as he hurtled downward. His muscular body rotated through the air, somehow managing to straighten itself out in time to slice the water cleanly.

A collective sigh went up from all the guests, followed by scattered applause. Ben was among those who clapped the loudest.

"I really don't think you should encourage him, Ben," Nancy warned. "Some day Patrick's urge to show off for Mary Ellen is going to get him badly hurt."

Ben's hawklike eyes glared at her. "Don't be such a goody-goody," he said. "For a girl who looks like dynamite, you can certainly act like a wet blanket at times."

"You're just saying that because you're angry," Nancy shot back. "Anyway, it isn't true! You're not being fair!"

"Fair!!" Ben pounced on the word almost glee-fully. "That's another fixation you have. Every-thing is supposed to be nice and neat and, above all, fair. Except fairness to you means that you get your way one hundred percent of the time."

Swallowing her anger, Nancy tried to steer the conversation back to the original subject. "I don't think I was asking so much," she said. "All I wanted was for you to come to dinner at my house. Just once. Is that such a big favor to ask? Most people like to get invited places. It isn't as if I'm asking you to go through some hideous ordeal. My parents are nice people."

"But I'm not dating your parents. I'm dating you," Ben countered.

"So what?"

"Your folks don't like me. That's so what. They just invited me so they can have a chance to do their disapproving at close range. I don't know what the problem is. Maybe it's because I'm not Jewish. . . ."

"It isn't that," Nancy said a bit too quickly.

"So what is it then?" Ben shot back. "I guess I'm just not the type they approve of. Too street-wise and tough for their little girl. You know damn well they'd rather you were still going out with that Josh Breitman."

"Leave Josh out of this," Nancy snapped. "At least he never got nasty just because I wanted him to come home to dinner. Josh was always nice and polite and — "

"And fair?" Ben asked, cocking one eyebrow sarcastically.

20

That was too much. "You want to see dynamite? I'll show you dynamite!" Nancy shouted. Without further warning she shot both arms out in front of her and lunged at Ben, pushing him straight-armed right to the edge of the pool.

Caught off balance, Ben teetered on the brink of the ledge, trying to stay upright. But there wasn't enough room for him to get a toehold. After a few seconds of futile resistance, Ben went flying into the water, all six-and-a-half feet of his body windmilling through the air.

As Ben righted himself and came sputtering up for breath, Nancy glared down at him triumphantly. "Now who's all wet?" she said.

Ben looked as if he might be ready to laugh and make up, putting the whole pointless argument behind them. But Nancy was in no mood for that. Suddenly tired of Ben and the whole party, she stalked away in a huff.

Claudia Randall had been watching the goings on with amusement while Pres gave a running commentary on the cast of characters.

"Your cheerleader friends certainly are feisty, aren't they?" she said with evident approval. "It's been quite a while since I've been anywhere where there was so much excitement."

Pres felt that this was his cue to ask Claudia what she was doing in Tarenton. So far he'd been doing the lion's share of the talking. About the only thing he knew about Claudia, aside from the fact that she was a Randall, was that she was eighteen years old. Had she graduated from high school yet? Was she working somewhere in town? Or was she a student?

As much as he was dying to know, Claudia's wistful tone of voice also reminded him that he'd kept her occupied talking for a long time. "Speaking of excitement," he said, "would you like to come for a swim? It isn't fair of me to keep talking to you all evening. You haven't even had a chance to try out the pool."

Claudia's violet eyes flashed. "Why, Pres Tilford, I'm surprised at you!" she exclaimed in mock horror. "Paddling around in the pool is kid stuff. If it's excitement you have in mind, I can think of better things to do."

Pres's jaw dropped. "You can?" He wasn't used to being with a girl who moved so fast she outpaced even his active imagination.

"What I would like is for us to take our own private tour of the rest of the new wing of the building," Claudia suggested. "There's a sauna. A lounge, everything. We could have it all to ourselves."

Pres nodded his head. "Good idea. But I'm sure it's locked."

"Oh, it is. But I had the foresight to borrow the key from the office bulletin board." Reaching into the pocket of her safari shirt, Claudia produced a ring of official-looking keys and dangled it under Pres's nose. "How about it? All we have to do is make sure no one notices us."

Unobtrusively, they wandered out into the hall and stood by the water fountain. They waited until they were sure there was no one in the rest rooms who might come out and see them, and no one watching from the area by the pool. Then Claudia deftly tried the keys one by one until she found the one that fit into the lock of the main entrance to the rest of the wing. The door opened and they both slipped in very quickly, shutting it behind them, and waited breathlessly for any indication that they'd been seen.

Apart from the muffled noises of the party, there wasn't a sound.

"We did it!" Pres gasped.

"Aren't we clever!" Claudia giggled.

Impulsively, she pulled Pres's head down to her level and kissed him. Her body, cool and elegant, yet eager, too, pressed against his.

"I hope you won't think I'm too terribly forward," Claudia said finally, her southern drawl returning to full strength. "But I get bored with flirting when it drags on too long. Live for today, that's my motto."

"I don't mind at all," Pres said, thinking he'd never heard anything truer in his entire life.

He bent down to kiss Claudia again and felt as if he were diving headfirst into those incredible amethyst-colored eyes. They look almost deep enough to drown in, he thought irrationally. But what a way to go!

CHAPTER

If her timing had been different by just a few seconds, Nancy Goldstein would have reached the hallway just in time to see Pres and Claudia sneaking into the locked wing of the Y. As it was, she was heading toward the water fountain at a good pace when she ran smack into Walt Manners.

Lost without Olivia at his side, Walt had arrived at the pool party late and then spent most of the evening hanging around aimlessly in the general area of the coat room. He'd been wondering how soon he could politely call it quits and go home, when Nancy came charging around the corner and collided with him, knocking them both into the heavily loaded coat rack.

After they'd dug themselves out from under a pile of down jackets and pea coats, Walt helped Nancy to her feet and started replacing the coats on their hangers. "This is the most interesting thing I've done all evening," he groused. "Dull party, isn't it?'

"I don't know. It looked like fun to me. Or it would have been, if Ben Adamson didn't insist on spoiling everything."

"Have a fight?" Walt asked unnecessarily.

"Did we ever!"

"Well, I'm sure you'll make up before the evening's over," Walt said.

"Not on your life," Nancy vowed. "That's just what Ben is counting on. He thinks he can give me a hard time all evening, and then when the party's finished we'll make up in time for a little cozy make-out session before we go home. For once, I'm going to show him he can't get away with it."

"So how are you getting home then?"

Nancy was taken aback. "I hadn't thought that far ahead. I have no idea."

"I'm leaving soon, if you want a lift," Walt offered.

"That would be great," Nancy said. "Let's get dressed and I'll meet you back here in a couple of minutes."

Nancy put her street clothes on as quickly as possible, but Walt was even speedier. When she left the women's changing room, Nancy saw him waiting over by the coat room, already bundled up in his down coat and plaid cap. She made a point of passing by Ben without so much as a good-bye on her way to the exit.

Reaching Walt's side, she couldn't help noticing that Vanessa Barlow, Tarenton High's champion gossip, was watching them with interest, from a spot just outside the coat room.

If Vanessa wants something to gossip about I might as well give it to her, Nancy thought rebelliously. It will serve Ben right for calling me dull.

Nancy gave Walt a hug that was a little more than just friendly and began adjusting the set of his plaid hunting cap. Walt didn't suspect that the gesture was anything more than a little playful, but Nancy knew that Vanessa, who had a lurid imagination, would think she was witnessing a romantic moment.

"Come on, Walt," Nancy said in a voice she calculated would be loud enough to overhear, "let's get out of this place. Just the two of us."

Once they'd driven away from the Y and reached the highway, Nancy began to wonder whether leaving the party so early had been a good idea.

One thing about her parents, they weren't stupid. If she showed up at home this early, and with someone other than Ben driving her, they were sure to guess that she and Ben had quarreled. They'd be right, naturally, but Nancy was in no hurry to give her folks another excuse for telling her that Ben was no good for her.

"You know what would save this evening from being a total disaster?" Nancy said out loud. "A big, gooey pizza with pepperoni and olives and extra cheese."

"And anchovies," said Walt. "If your girl friend goes out of town and leaves you feeling lonely, at least there's always anchovies."

"And onions," Nancy giggled. "Lots and lots of onions without having to worry about what they'll do to your breath."

"I knew you were smart," Walt said, "but this is the first time I ever realized what a genius you are."

They reached the Pizza Palace just in time to get their order in before the kitchen closed. "You'll have to make that pie an order to go, though," the counter boy warned. "The place is dead tonight so we're closing down early."

The pie smelled delicious, but by the time they'd paid the bill the cook was shutting down the oven.

Just as they settled down in the jeep and started to open up the pizza box, the parking lot floodlights were switched off. "Something tells me that's a none too subtle hint," Walt said. "I guess the Pizza Palace doesn't want us picnicking in their parking lot."

"So now what?" said Nancy. "We could go to my house I guess, but by the time we get there this food will be cold."

"Ditto," said Walt.

"I have an idea," he added after a pause. "But promise not to take it the wrong way. Okay? We could go to the Overlook."

The Overlook, with its picturesque view of Narrow Brook Lake, illuminated at night by the lights of the houses lining the shore, was a notorious parking spot. "I'm not trying to put a move on you. Honest," Walt promised. "At the moment the only thing I'm lusting over is this pizza."

"Sounds perfect," Nancy agreed. "Let's get going."

In between wolfing down slices of pizza, Nancy and Walt commiserated on the failure of the evening.

"I've gotten to the point where I just don't feel like myself when Olivia's not around," Walt confessed. "I hate myself for admitting it. I've always prided myself on being the independent type and all that."

"It doesn't sound too bad to me," Nancy said. "All it means is that you and Olivia share something special. You communicate. With Ben, I've got problems both ways. I'm miserable when he's not around. And lately, I seem to be miserable when he's around, too. Sometimes, for no reason at all, Ben starts acting as if he hates me."

Nancy summarized her latest fight with Ben for Walt's benefit. "We were just having a little discussion and all of a sudden he started calling me names. Wet blanket! Why doesn't he just call me a witch? Making fun of me for wanting things to be 'fair' is even worse. What am I supposed to say? That I don't want to be fair?"

"Maybe," Walt suggested, "Ben is just afraid of being rejected. He wants to hang on to his advantage by threatening to reject you first."

"But why? I'm crazy about him. Why is wanting him to come to my house for dinner a sign of rejection?"

Walt chewed ruminatively on his last slice of pizza. "It's hard to explain, Nancy. But you're so . . . so perfect. Your looks are perfect. Your clothes. Your grades. You live in a house that looks like something out of a magazine. Y'know, I've been there for parties and I've never seen a house like that before.

"Even Pres's place, which is bigger and a lot more expensive, I guess, is filled with stuff that was bought at all different times. Some valuable antiques. Some new stuff. His mother's ghastly needlepoints thrown over a chair that would probably be worth enough to pay my college tuition. . . . They've even got family heirlooms around, like those portraits of the original Til-fords, which, personally, I'd throw out in the trash.

"Anyway, as I was saying, your house is the only house I know of in Tarenton where *every-thing* matches. It's color and style coordinated right down to the knickknacks. I bet it scares Ben half to death. You know, it's like one of those picture puzzles they used to give you back in grade school: 'What's wrong with this pic-ture?' And Ben can guess the answer with no trouble at all. It's him. He's the one thing in your life that doesn't fit the picture."

Nancy thought this over for a while. She wanted to say it was all wrong, but it made all too much sense.

29

"But what am I supposed to do?" she asked, her eyes tearing up. "When I try to be nice to Ben, to reassure him that it's okay, he acts like he hates me. It almost seems like he's most interested in me when I'm being . . . well, witchy."

They both thought of the phrase at the same time: "Life sure is confusing, ain't it," they said in perfect unison.

It was something Coach Engborg said often when things got impossibly snarled up. At the beginning of the year the whole squad had groaned over the dreadful cliché. Now some of them were starting to pick up the habit of using it.

Walt laughed. "Great minds think alike," he said.

"At least we had the timing right that time," Nancy agreed. "Our timing was perfect."

"DON'T MAKE ANY SUDDEN MOVES. GET OUT OF THE CAR VERY SLOWLY, KEEPING YOUR HANDS IN VIEW AT ALL TIMES."

The voice, electronically amplified, enveloped the jeep and penetrated right through to their very bones.

Nancy felt as if the wind had been knocked out of her. "Oh no," she wailed, barely loud enough for Walt to hear. "We're going to be robbed. Or worse!" Reflexively, she started grabbing for her purse, which was on the floor beside her.

"I wouldn't do that," Walt warned. He said the

words very slowly and deliberately, but Nancy could hear the tension underneath.

"Do exactly what they say." Walt went on. "Keep your hands in view. They'll think you're going for a gun.

"It's okay, though," he added. "It's only the State Patrol."

Only!

Nancy had never been in a situation remotely like this before, and relieved as she was that she wasn't going to be robbed and assaulted, being pulled from a car at gunpoint by the State Patrol was only slightly less terrifying.

They got out of the car very carefully.

One of the officers — a huge, burly man — pushed Walt against the side of the car and began patting him down for weapons.

The other one, who was much younger, seemed vaguely embarrassed as he glanced inside Nancy's purse to check for a weapon. "We weren't doing anything, honestly," Nancy kept trying to explain. "We didn't come up here to make out. We were just eating pizza. . . ."

The younger officer had to struggle to keep a straight face.

Of course he doesn't believe that one, Nancy thought. Why should he? She knew she was making a fool of herself. She ought to just shut up. But she was so nervous that she wanted to keep jabbering on. "We're not going to be arrested are we?" she pleaded. "My parents would just die. . . ."

"If you'll be quiet a minute, young lady, you

might find out," the huge officer said finally.

Then, ignoring Nancy completely, he turned to Walt and demanded to see some identification. At the sight of the name and address on Walt's driver's license, his eyes bulged slightly. "Don't tell me you're the kid of the people on TV!" he said, almost as if Walt were trying to pull a fast one on him.

"I am. Honest injun," Walt said. " 'Breakfast at Home' — those are my parents."

"Okay. Want to tell me what you did this evening?"

"It's like Nancy said," Walt replied. He explained how they'd left the pool party early, then gone for pizza, and ended up at the Overlook because the Pizza Palace was closing.

The officer peered inside the jeep and confirmed the existence of an empty pizza box on the seat. Suddenly he seemed bored, as if Walt and Nancy had tricked him into wasting his time.

"All right, all right," he said. "But I've got to take you kids down to the village police station. There's been a burglary, and Sergeant Danielli down there will want statements from you as part of his investigation."

Burglary! Nancy and Walt exchanged puzzled glances as they got into the backseat of the State Patrol car. The young officer, driving Walt's jeep, followed them as they headed into the center of the village.

Sergeant Danielli was a lot more understanding. The second-in-command of the five-person

Tarenton area police force knew both Walt's and Nancy's parents. While he got Walt to repeat his story about his whereabouts that evening, he sent Nancy out to the outer office, to wait with the woman civilian who ran the switchboard.

"Are you sure you didn't drive down into the village after the party?" Danielli asked skeptically when Walt had finished his story. "I don't see you as a burglar, but sometimes high spirits can get out of hand. You know, maybe you have a drink and want to impress your girl friend. If that's what it's all about, you might as well tell the truth."

Walt was baffled. "I don't have any idea what this is all about," he insisted. "We weren't drinking. And besides, Nancy isn't even my girl friend. Ask her. Ask anybody."

Sergeant Danielli sighed. "Okay, okay. If Johnny Rush, the Pizza Palace night manager, confirms your story, then we'll forget the whole thing. Why don't you go out and wait with the girl while I make a few calls?"

Outside, Nancy pulled Walt down to the end of the waiting room benches, out of earshot of the switchboard operator, and filled him in on what she'd learned from her.

"I don't think she was supposed to tell me," Nancy said, "but I guess it's about the weirdest thing that has happened on the Tarenton crime scene in years. Do you know old Mrs. Rogers?"

"Sure," Walt said. "She's about ninety years

old and drives that ancient Nash Rambler. Her car alone is older than I am. Who doesn't know her?"

"Well, she was driving through the village at about quarter to eleven tonight," Nancy said, "and she saw some guy in a jeep just like yours stop in front of Tatum's Jewelry Store and smash the display window with a baseball bat. Fortunately, she scared the guy away before he could take much."

"You mean, Mrs. Rogers went after the burglar herself?" Walt asked in amazement.

Nancy giggled. "Not quite. You know how that car of hers backfires all the time. It makes an awful racket. Well, I guess she got nervous and stalled it, and then when she started it up again the engine was backfiring like crazy. The burglar thought it was gunfire and took off."

Walt grinned. "They ought to give the car a medal or something. But who could it have been? I don't know of another jeep like mine in town. It's an old model and it's got those silver glow-in-the dark decal stripes all over it. I put them on because Mom was always worried she'd back into it at night, when she tried to get her car out of the driveway."

Nancy grimaced. "Exactly. Mrs. Rogers didn't get a license number. But her description fit your jeep to a T."

While they were talking, the two State Patrol officers returned and went inside Sergeant Danielli's office. This time, the door was left open, and Walt and Nancy could hear the officers lecturing

34

Danielli about the Tarenton population's lack of concern for security. "After this, at least maybe Harry Tatum will have the sense to get an iron gate," the officer said. "Or at least empty the display window when he closes up."

Sergeant Danielli was unimpressed. "Come on now, boys. This isn't the big city. Besides, Tatum lives right over the store. He was there in five minutes, and according to him, nothing of value was taken except one ring." He ruffled through some papers looking for the report. "A Gemini birthstone ring set with diamond chips and rubies. Value about seven hundred dollars, but it's going to be just about impossible for the thief to get rid of it. It's a pretty memorable description and we'll have it all over the state by tomorrow.

"We do appreciate your efforts," Danielli told the pair. "Even though you got the wrong kid."

"You sure about that?" the older officer asked.

"Well," said Danielli, "the Pizza Palace manager says they came in just before eleven and picked up a large pie with all the trimmings. It doesn't figure that they would have raced down to the village and attempted a burglary fifteen minutes later. Then they would have had to hightail it out to the Overlook and wolf down the food by the time you guys found them there. It doesn't make sense. Besides, Mrs. Rogers only saw the one young man. Where was the girl?"

The State Patrolmen seemed dubious. "It could be, or maybe they were just trying to establish an alibi."

Sergeant Danielli sighed. "You guys are watching too much TV. I've wasted enough time on this."

Rising from his desk, he went over to the glass partition that separated his office from the outer waiting area and tapped on the window. "You kids can go home now. Get outta here. We're finished with you," he grumbled, not unkindly.

Nancy felt relief flooding over her. "I can't believe it! This means they're not going to call our parents. My dad would have had a heart attack if he got a call saying I was in custody at the police station. I'd never hear the end of it, even if it was just some big mistake."

Walt squeezed Nancy's arm. "Don't worry. It's still only a little after midnight. I'll take you right home.

"I can't think of a single reason," he added, "why your folks should ever have to know about this."

CHAPTER

4

Walt and Nancy stepped out the police station doors and into the glare of a bank of floodlights.

Blinking in astonishment, they both suddenly knew how a deer must feel when it was hypnotized by the high beams of a car. Momentarily blinded, they felt paralyzed as well, helpless to escape whatever it was that was happening to them.

After a confusing few seconds they were dimly aware that they were surrounded by at least four people. One of them stuck a microphone under their noses and started shouting at them:

"Is it true that you were just questioned as suspects in the Tatum burglary?

"How does it feel to be the son of the ideal TV couple and find yourself in this fix?" the voice asked Walt.

"Are you the girl friend?" a voice asked Nancy. "What were you doing at the Overlook after it happened?"

Nancy felt the fear ebb and indignation take its place. All evening, it seemed, people had been pushing her around and accusing her of dumb things. "Leave us alone," she shouted, her eyes brimming with tears of anger. "You've got it all wrong. We were at a pool party and we left early. Then we were hungry and we went up to the Overlook to eat pizza. That's all. We're not guilty. . . ."

Dimly she remembered something she'd overheard Sergeant Danielli telling the State Patrol officers in his office. "We're not crooks," she added angrily. "We've got an alibi!"

Walt grabbed her arm and forcibly dragged her away in the direction of the jeep. "Just shut up," he yelled. "You're only making things worse!"

Inside the jeep, he apologized. "I'm sorry for talking to you that way, but you don't know how they're going to make that sound."

Nancy was horrified. "You don't mean they'll use that?"

"I'm afraid they probably will."

Actually, Walt knew it was more than probable. His own parents were in TV, and he could see that Nancy's outburst, innocent as it may have been, was going to make a terrific story. On videotape, her anger would look more like guilt and hysteria.

"But how did they find out we were there?"

Nancy wanted to know. "And won't the police tell them it was all a mistake?"

"The answer to the first question," Walt explained, "is that they were probably listening in on the police frequency. It's done all the time. Unfortunately, that was the crew from Channel Eight. They've been trying to lure my parents over to their station for years. Their news manager will be only too glad to be able to get back at my folks. After all, they're his competition.

"As for your second question," Walt went on, "Sergeant Danielli is sure to tell them it was all a mistake. But he'd probably say the same thing if he thought I was guilty, and just didn't have enough evidence to arrest us. So you can hardly blame the reporter if he doesn't believe it. For once, I'm sorry we're over sixteen. If we weren't, then they couldn't use our names."

Nancy groaned. "How am I ever going to explain this to my folks? I'm not even supposed to be at the Overlook. They never said in so many words that I wasn't allowed, but you know how parents are. It probably never occurred to them that I would, even though they know very well that everyone else our age does."

"If you want I'll come in with you when I take you home now and back up your story," Walt volunteered.

"Somehow," Nancy said, "I don't think the word of another burglary suspect is going to impress my mom and dad. You better let me handle this alone.

"At least," she added, "I wasn't with Ben. If

I'd been with him, my parents would never have believed we were innocent in a million years."

The thought was only momentarily comforting. It had occurred to Nancy that Ben watched TV news, too.

Luckily for Nancy, her parents took her side. Mr. and Mrs. Goldstein were so outraged that their daughter had been hauled down to the police station like a common criminal, and then harrassed by reporters, that they momentarily forgot the part about her being at the Overlook when it happened.

Nancy suspected that in a few days, when they calmed down, their attitude might change. But for the moment, they were completely sympathetic.

Ben's reaction was something else.

Ben called the Goldstein house the next morning, and at first he seemed furious. "It's bad enough that you had to walk out on me in front of all those people," he raved. "But then you have to get yourself on TV, so that the whole town knows you finished off the evening with another guy. Good work, Nancy!"

Nancy didn't say much. She was in no mood to apologize to Ben.

Eventually, however, he calmed down on his own. "I've got to hand it to you," he said, breaking into a chuckle. "That line about going up to the Overlook to eat pizza was really something. Only you would be straight-arrow enough to think that anyone could possibly believe that.

And the rest of it was pretty good, too. 'We're not guilty. We have an alibi!' " Ben imitated Nancy's high-pitched denial. "I don't think I ever laughed so hard!"

Nancy was in no mood to see the humor in the situation. "I'm glad it was amusing to you," she said angrily. "I would think, though, that you might stop to think how it all made me feel."

"Of course I'm sympathetic," Ben protested. "But there was no lasting harm done. And you really did look kind of cute and feisty telling off that vulture of a reporter."

Cute! "I'm in no mood for this talk, Ben," Nancy said. "It had nothing to do with cute. So just get lost. Okay?"

Nancy slammed down the phone, and stalked upstairs to her bedroom. Ben was jealous of Walt, all right, but aside from that, she seemed almost secretly glad that the whole mess had happened. Maybe Walt had been right. Ben had felt that Nancy was up there on a pedestal, but now she'd been knocked down a peg. Now that her life wasn't perfectly under control, he felt that they were more . . . equal.

That's fine for Ben, Nancy told herself, but what about me? I need a boyfriend who'll be supportive. Not someone who's secretly glad to see me messing up.

Nancy flung herself down on her bed. She loved her room and the way she and her mother had fixed it up. Normally, it made her feel calm and happy, her own special retreat that nothing could spoil. The color scheme was peach and ivory. A peach satin bedspread. Ivory sheets with peach-colored initials embroidered on the hems. Peach drapes. Ivory wall paper with a tiny print, very subdued, in peach.

As much as she didn't care to see Ben's point of view at the moment, she couldn't help thinking about her conversation with Walt before the police showed up last night.

There was something a little bit excessive about her house. No wonder it made Ben nervous. She could imagine that someone who wasn't used to it might feel a bit claustrophobic. Everything was so planned out it was almost smothering.

Smothered was exactly how Olivia had felt all Friday evening. Her mother and father had picked her up in the car immediately after the game, and they'd driven until after midnight, trying to make good mileage while the traffic was light.

Unfortunately, Mr. Evans had done all the driving, which left her mother free to think about things to worry about.

Mrs. Evans had started out worrying that the wedding present they'd bought for cousin Jessie wasn't expensive enough. Then she'd worried that it was too expensive. She'd interrogated Olivia about the dress she'd brought to wear to the reception and criticized her choice. And finally, when Olivia tried to cut the conversation short by pretending to sleep, she'd started in on her favorite theme of Olivia's health.

Cheering at the game had obviously worn her out, Mrs. Evans said, otherwise Olivia wouldn't look so washed out and pale.

"Mom, I'm fine," Olivia protested wearily. "I just need a little peace and quiet. Puh-leeze."

"Well, if my own daughter can't stand to talk to me, I don't know what I'm going to do. Who am I supposed to talk to?" Mrs. Evans had mumbled before settling into an offended silence.

That was pretty typical of how things usually worked out when Olivia had to spend a lot of time alone with her parents. Her mother nagged her until she snapped back. But in the end, Olivia always ended up being the one to feel guilty. After all, Olivia had been pretty sickly as a child. She'd had operations on her heart, and there had been times when the doctors were ready to give up on her. Through it all, her mom had been constantly at her side, taking care of her. So it seemed ungrateful to resent her now for being overprotective.

And besides, Olivia felt bad for her father, who said little but always looked so hurt when she and Mom started in on each other.

For the rest of the evening, Olivia managed to hold her tongue. By the time they'd checked into the motel, however, she was too nervous to sleep. She'd lain awake half the night, afraid to get up because she might wake her folks from their sound sleep.

When sunrise came, she was awake again, after two or three hours of tossing and turning. As quietly as possible, she pulled on her clothes and went out for an early morning jog around the parking lot.

After that, she had no idea what she'd do. Her parents wouldn't be awake for hours yet, and it was too dark inside the room to read without a light. Jogging past the brightly lit motel lobby, she saw a sign advertising free orange juice, tea, and coffee. Happy for an excuse to hang around inside, she went in and got herself a glass of juice, then sat down in front of the huge TV screen, which was tuned to the early morning news.

"And now a report from our sister station, Channel Eight in Grove Lake," the announcer was saying. "It seems the son of two popular local TV personalities, known for their advocacy of family values and wholesome outdoor living, was questioned by police last night, along with his girl friend, in connection with a jewelry store burglary."

Olivia's first thought was that it must be some kind of weird coincidence. The description sounded like Walt. The person shown in the video film clip even looked like Walt. He was wearing the same kind of plaid hunting cap and dark-rimmed glasses.

But, of course, it couldn't actually *be* Walt.

For one thing, the announcer said he'd been questioned along with his girl friend, and that had never happened.

"I'm right here," Olivia said, talking back to the screen.

Then, as the clip rolled on, it dawned on Olivia that it wasn't a mistake. And it wasn't a dream either. She recognized Walt's round face, looking startled and angry. And then, as the TV camera zoomed in on the face of the "girl friend," she realized it was Nancy Goldstein, her voice quivering in indignation.

"We were at a pool party and we left early," Nancy was saying. "The Overlook to eat pizza." Then, "We're not guilty. . . . We've got an alibi!"

What was it all about? Walt in jail? Walt and Nancy at the Overlook together?

Olivia pulled herself together and got some change for the pay phone from the desk clerk. She dialed the Manners' number and got a busy signal.

Between then and nine o'clock, when her parents got up, she must have tried calling back at least ten times. Eventually, she realized that Walt's family had probably taken the phone off the hook. After that report they must be getting dozens of calls that they'd prefer not to answer.

At first, she'd just felt scared and worried on Walt's behalf. The more she tried to get through to him without success, the more she realized that she was also hurt and angry. She'd only been out of town a few hours, and already Walt was hanging around with Nancy. Any boy who was that much of a skunk deserved all the trouble he was in!

CHAPTER

"**P**oor Walt! Imagine! He wanted to impress Nancy so badly, and the only thing he could think of to do was to rob a jewelry store for her!"

In spite of her words of pity, Vanessa Barlow looked delighted. Her plum-colored, talon-length fingernails gleamed as she reenacted the crime by pretending to smash in the window of the Pineland Mall Bakery with an imaginary bat.

"Burglary," said Shelley Eismar. "In the first place, it was burglary. Not a robbery."

Vanessa looked annoyed. She hated to be interrupted when she was on a roll. "Whatever. Anyway, the real irony is that he should have done it for Olivia. I mean, Nancy Goldstein has scads of jewelry. Olivia is the one who dresses like an orphan. She could use the help."

The Eismar twins exchanged disgusted glances. Not that much exciting happened around Tarenton, and the story of Walt and Nancy getting pulled into the police station was too juicy to be forgotten anytime soon. But Vanessa was enjoying it all too much. Besides being inaccurate.

"No one thinks Walt really did it," Cathleen Eismar pointed out. "Aren't you getting a little bit carried away?"

Vanessa grinned her Cheshire Cat grin. "But you didn't see what I saw."

The Eimars looked at each other again. They didn't want to encourage Vanessa, but neither of them could resist the temptation to get the scoop on what really happened. One way or another, Vanessa sometimes did know things other people didn't.

"Okay," said Shelley, "we're hooked. So tell us."

"Weeelll," Vanessa said, "at the pool party, the two of them were thrashing around on the floor under this big pile of coats. They must have been drinking on the sly, I guess, and just got carried away. Then Nancy was hanging all over Walt. I heard her tell him that she wanted him to take her somewhere so they could be alone. Just the two of them."

The Eismars considered this information.

"It's a good story," said Shelley, "but I don't believe it. Not about those two."

"It's true, though," Vanessa insisted. "And I'm going to make sure my father hears about it. After all, he's the superintendent of schools, so he's got to take some action. The members of the cheerleading squad are supposed to represent the school. This scandal, on TV and all, reflects on all of us."

"You mean he doesn't know already?" Cathleen asked. "It only happened last night, but it was on Channel Eight news at least three times today."

"Dad's away at some golf tournament this weekend, but when he gets back he'll blow his stack. He always asks me to keep him up-to-date on anything that affects the school."

The Eismars' father worked in the school system, too, so they knew that this last part wasn't just an empty boast.

"Did it ever strike you as bizarre," Shelley said to her sister after Vanessa left, "that the superintendent of schools gets most of his information about what goes on at Tarenton High from *her*? That's sort of like a heart surgeon going to Dracula to learn about blood."

"Vampira," corrected Cathleen. "Vanessa should change her name.

"If I thought the students at Tarenton were all like Vanessa," Cathleen added, "I wouldn't *want* to be superintendent of schools."

"Or maybe you'd just be more likely to believe Vanessa, when she bad-mouthed other kids," Shelley suggested. "It can't be easy to admit to yourself that you've fathered a monster."

"Still," Cathleen said, as they headed back to their car, "you can't help wondering if there's any truth to that coat room story. I don't think Walt is the jewelry store burglar or anything like that. But they did go up to the Overlook. . . ."

Shelley giggled. "It is kind of funny when you think about it. Look at all the couples who stop there all the time and no one's the wiser. Then Walt and Nancy try to sneak off without their steadies knowing about it and they end up on TV."

"It's true," Cathleen agreed. "I wouldn't like to be in their shoes now. They're both going to have a lot of explaining to do."

On Monday before practice, Walt went into Coach Engborg's office and volunteered to leave the squad, at least until the real burglar was caught. "I didn't do anything wrong," he told the coach, "but I can see how embarrassing it could be to have me representing the school."

"Don't be foolish," Ardith Engborg said. "Haven't you ever heard that we're all innocent until proven guilty? And in this case, there isn't even a charge against you. I set high standards for my cheerleaders, but I'm not going to have you going into hiding because of gossip. If you're right, fight, that's what I always say."

Walt felt better for the first time all day. "I really appreciate this, Coach," he said.

"Just one thing, Walt," Ardith said before he could leave her office. "If you don't mind, I think we'll give the wolf outfit a little rest for a few weeks."

"But why?" No sooner had the words left his mouth than Walt figured out the answer and felt his ears redden with embarrassment.

Ardith grinned.

"Okay," Walt mumbled as he fled the room. "Whatever you say."

All in all, Walt had to admit to himself, Coach Engborg had been a lot more understanding than Olivia.

He'd had no way of getting in touch with Olivia over the weekend because he didn't know her cousin's address. In any case, it had never occurred to him that the news report would get beyond Channel Eight. When he did learn that it had been broadcast all over the tri-state area, because of his parents' being so well-known, there was nothing he could do anyway.

On Sunday, when he called the Evans' house, Olivia and her family still weren't back from their trip. So he'd had to catch up with her in the hall the next morning, not exactly an ideal place for discussing a sensitive subject.

As soon as he saw Olivia's face, he'd known that the discussion was going to be difficult for more reasons than one. Olivia had that closed up look that she wore when she was trying hard to keep her emotions under control.

"Livvy, I can explain everything," he'd told her. "It was just a case of mistaken identity. And the only reason it got on the news was because Channel Eight wanted to embarrass my parents."

"Mistaken identity!" Olivia said. "I suppose it was mistaken identity that caused you to end up at the Overlook with Nancy instead of me!"

"Of course not," said Walt. "I was talking

about the other part. About getting hauled in by the cops."

Olivia made a gesture with her hand that dismissed that whole part of the story. "I don't care about that stuff. I believe you on that. And even if you did it, I'm not sure I'd really care. The only thing that really bothers me is why you were with Nancy."

Walt scratched his head. Sometimes he couldn't figure Olivia out. "But that was totally innocent," he said. "We were just talking."

Now Olivia looked really suspicious. Worse than if he'd confessed to some horrible crime. "Talking about what?" she demanded.

"Nothing," shrugged Walt. "You know, things. Problems. Relationships. That kind of junk."

"Junk like your relationship with me, for instance?"

Walt knew he was sunk. He never could deal with this kind of argument. He lost every time. "It wasn't the way you make it sound."

"I bet. I'm not out of town four hours and you and Nancy are parked at the Overlook, having a heart-to-heart talk about your problems with me, and hers with Ben. And all you can say is, 'It wasn't that way.'"

"You bet it's all I can say. Because it's true," Walt shot back. "And if you don't want to believe it, then don't. I've got enough problems without worrying about a so-called girl friend who doesn't trust me."

* * *

Surprisingly, practice that day didn't go badly.

No one wanted to talk about what had happened, so the whole squad concentrated hard on what they were doing. And Ardith, sensing the need to keep everyone occupied, announced a different routine than usual.

"We've reached that point in the year when I think you know the cheers and routines backward and forward," she said. "But I worry that it's all starting to become a little mechanical. So we'll spend the first part of the practice on shape-up routines, and then we'll do some ballet exercises. They're great for helping you to concentrate on your form."

Mary Ellen was so grateful to Coach Engborg for taking charge that she wished she could have hugged her. It was fine being squad captain and having partial responsibility for keeping things going during practice as long as everyone was getting along, but on days like this she felt like a nervous wreck.

Today, Walt and Olivia were obviously not speaking. Olivia and Nancy looked like they were just aching for a chance to tear each other apart. Pres was daydreaming, just walking around with a big grin on his face, like a kid who'd just found out where his parents were hiding the Christmas presents. And Angie was depressed. In other words, it was a fairly typical bad day for the Tarenton High Cheerleading Squad.

"All right, troops," shouted Ardith, "let's start off with twenty-five laps around the gym, just to get our circulation going."

52

Everyone groaned, especially Mary Ellen and Pres, the two members of the squad who happened to be allergic to unnecessary physical exercise.

"I don't know how you do it," Mary Ellen said to Angie, who sprinted her laps without difficulty, honey-blonde hair flying, and ended up looking as fresh as when she started. "For someone who hates sports and is always pigging out on chocolate, you sure have a lot of energy."

Angie smiled to herself, then frowned. Mary Ellen's remark was certainly a backhanded compliment if there ever was one. It's my own fault, though, Angie told herself. She was always making jokes about her bad habits, like her addiction to sweets, but she kept her good ones, like jogging, a well-kept secret. If people believed the image she set up for herself, could she really blame them?

After the laps, Ardith led the squad in a vigorous twenty-five minutes of aerobics that left everyone too winded to worry about personal differences. Then, she spent some time reviewing basic ballet positions. "I'm not planning to turn you all into ballet dancers," she explained, "but practicing these positions will make you more conscious of how you move."

Nancy and Olivia had both taken ballet when they were kids, and found it fun to be going over exercises they had learned years before. The other girls and Walt, who'd taken modern dance and tap but never ballet, found themselves challenged to keep up. And even Pres, who might normally have made a fuss over doing something that threatened his macho self-image, was starting to enjoy himself.

This is too good to be true, Mary Ellen muttered to herself as she watched the others struggling to copy Ardith's graceful arm and hand movements.

No sooner had she had the thought, than the double doors to the gym swung open, and Ben Adamson appeared. He stood, out of sight of the others, with his arms folded across his chest. With his slightly stoop-shouldered posture and beaky nose, Ben had always reminded Mary Ellen a little bit of a vulture. And never more than today.

As soon as Ardith announced the end of the practice, Ben stepped out into full view. "Hey, Nance," he called out, "I need to talk to you."

Nancy was in no mood. The more she thought about it, the more she blamed Ben for the way Friday night had turned out. If he hadn't picked a fight in the first place, none of it would have ever happened. "Well, I don't want to talk to you," she called back across the floor.

Ben reddened. He hadn't counted on being snubbed in front of the whole squad. "Oh, come on, Nancy. It won't hurt you to talk to me for a couple of minutes. Whadya say?"

"She *said* she didn't want to talk to you!" Walt's voice vibrated with challenge. He bounded across the floor and confronted Ben, mimicking his crossed-arm stance.

Unfortunately for Walt, he was nearly a foot shorter than Ben, so instead of meeting him eyeball to eyeball, he found himself staring at Ben's folded hands. Ben had a good view of the top of Walt's head. He looked half pained, half amused.

"Come on, Walt," he pleaded, "don't make a big deal of this. I just wanted to have a few words with my girl friend."

"She doesn't want any words with you. So get lost."

"Don't tell me to get lost, you — pipsqueak." Ben's midsentence glance in the direction of Coach Engborg served notice that he had a less polite word in mind, but was controlling himself in her presence.

Walt, though, would probably have rather been called anything but a pipsqueak. He reared back, ready to take a swing.

"Stop it, you guys." Nancy managed to get across the floor and in between the two boys so fast the others on the court weren't actually sure they'd seen her move.

"Thanks for coming to my defense, Walt," she said. "But it isn't really necessary." She gave Ben a cool look. "I'll talk to you for a couple of minutes," she told him. "But not here. Outside."

Ben shrugged and followed Nancy out the swinging doors. Walt, grumbling like a bear, shambled off in the direction of the boys' locker room.

Olivia was the first to reach the girls' changing room.

When Angie and Mary Ellen came in just behind her, too stunned to know what to say, Olivia turned on Angie and gave her a dirty look. "It's all your fault, Angie Poletti," she said accusingly.

Angie's jaw dropped. "Me! What did I do?"

" 'Lighten up, Livvy. What can happen in one weekend?' " Olivia said, imitating Angie's slightly throatier voice. "If you hadn't given me such bum advice, I'd have told my parents to go away without me. It seems to me that plenty happened."

Angie made a face. She knew that Olivia had argued with her parents about the trip and lost. "My advice had nothing to do with it," she retorted. "When are you going to grow up?"

Olivia pulled on her parka and stalked out of the locker room, still wearing her sweaty rehearsal clothes.

Angie turned to Mary Ellen and shrugged. "Can you beat that?" she asked.

"She didn't mean it," Mary Ellen said, not too convincingly. "But now that she's gone, tell me. What did you think of Walt's little scene out there? Seems to me he's hung up on Nancy after all. He's awfully jealous of Ben."

"I don't know about that," Angie ventured. "Maybe's it's just hurt pride."

"What do you mean?"

"Look at it this way," Angie said, "Walt offered to see Nancy home safely from the dance. Instead, just because she was with him, she ended up getting hauled down to the police station and embarrassed on the TV news. Maybe he just feels like a failure, and wants to make it up by being extra protective of Nancy."

"I don't know about that," Mary Ellen said.

56

She might believe something like that, if it were Patrick involved. But it was hard for her to imagine Walt almost provoking a fight just because his ego was bruised. He was such a happy-go-lucky guy normally.

"Well," she said, laughing, "one thing we know is that Walt would never have stolen anything from Tatum's. Most of their stuff is junk, anyway. And look what the thief took! A zodiac ring. Knowing Tatum's I bet it was really tacky!"

"Besides which," Angie added, "Walt happens to be a Capricorn. I remember, because he was one of the first kids in our class to turn sixteen and qualify for a driver's license. And I'm pretty sure Olivia is a Virgo, like me."

Mary Ellen looked impressed. Sometimes Angie thought of things that would never have occurred to her. "We ought to know Nancy's sign, too. She had a birthday party, remember."

"What difference does it make?" said Angie.

Mary Ellen sighed. "You're the one who brought the subject up. I'm just curious, that's all."

Angie thought. "I'm sure it must be some time during the second week of June," she said. "Because it was the same week school let out for summer vacation."

Mary Ellen spotted a day-old newspaper left behind on the shelf near the supply closet and started rummaging through the pages in search of the horoscope section. "Here it is," she said triumphantly, "Gemini. May 21 to June 21. Can you believe it? Nancy Goldstein is a Gemini!"

CHAPTER

Pres was feeling very pleased with himself.

For the first time since he could remember, luck seemed to be on his side. As much as he sympathized with Walt and Nancy, he couldn't help thinking that their timing had been a great break for him. Everyone was so busy gossiping about their little escapade that no one had time to wonder about who Claudia was, or to recall that she and Pres had disappeared early in the evening. Unbelievable as it seemed at the time, Claudia had been right when she promised him that they could sneak into the closed-off rooms of the health club and not get caught.

For once in his life, Pres thought, he was hung up on a girl who had more self-confidence than he did. With Claudia, there were none of the endless arguments about sex that had made his relationship with Kerry Elliot so tense. Kerry had been warm and loving, but for her the whole subject of physical contact had been boxed in by big words like commitment, and trust, and responsibility. Maybe it was because she was two years younger, or because she had never quite felt secure with a guy who had a reputation for getting around a lot, but she'd been skittish about getting too involved right from the very beginning.

With Claudia, there were no such hang-ups. Claudia knew exactly how far she was willing to go, and exactly where she was going to draw the line. And if anything, she seemed ready to get serious even faster than he would have tried to on his own. It was a little disorienting sometimes, being with a girl who didn't seem one bit concerned with the big "C" — COMMITMENT — but Pres was looking forward to getting used to it. He could do without the soul searching and all those agonizing, circular discussions that had always seemed to come up with Kerry every time he started feeling really sexy.

Of course, it wasn't only sex that attracted him to Claudia. He couldn't remember ever meeting a girl whom he had felt so close to so fast. Maybe it was because they had a lot in common in their backgrounds, but he felt that he could talk to her about a lot of things that normally he wouldn't share with a girl.

In fact, looking back on the past weekend, it almost seemed that he'd been talking nonstop ever since he and Claudia had met.

On Saturday, he'd met Claudia first thing in

the morning and taken her for a sightseeing tour of the area. They'd ended up going all the way to Loon Lake up in the mountains, and then stopped at a little roadside restaurant where they had a late lunch in a cozy room complete with a fireplace.

On the drive home, he'd actually let Claudia drive the Porsche — something he'd never done before with a date. Claudia enjoyed speed a little too much to be his idea of an ideal driver, but she had handled the car with confidence and skill. And it had been fun to see the mixture of concentration and sheer pleasure on her face, as she negotiated the winding country roads coming down the mountains.

On Sunday, he'd seen her again, and they'd ended up going out to the big monthly antiques fair over in Muskeagton. That was something else he'd never done with a date before. There were a couple of dealers who were regulars at the fair who specialized in antique silver, which happened to be a special interest of his — an interest he'd always been careful to keep from revealing to the other kids at Tarenton High. It was all very well to flaunt the family money by driving around in a Porsche, but admitting to an interest in antiques would have put him in danger of fitting the cliched image of the arrogant rich kid — something he'd always worked hard to avoid.

With Claudia, though, there seemed to be no need to worry about image. She knew a little bit about old china and glassware herself, and she didn't seem to think there was anything strange at all about a guy taking an interest in silverware.

Tonight, right after practice, he and Claudia were going to be having their fourth date in as many days. As he shifted into high gear and swung out onto the highway leading to Grove Lake, where Claudia was staying, Pres was elated at the prospect of seeing her again. The plan was for them to go back to his house and listen to records, especially some of the rare jazz records from his dad's collection that Claudia had expressed an interest in.

When he reached the outskirts of Grove Lake, Pres dug out the note he'd made of Claudia's address and began scanning the street signs carefully. This was the first time he'd come to pick Claudia up. He'd offered, but on their other dates so far she'd always had some reason to drive to Tarenton in her own car and meet him there.

Come to think of it, Pres thought idly, if there was anything that bothered him about Claudia it was that she was just a little bit too mysterious.

When they were together, he always felt that they were sharing so much, talking about everything under the sun with the greatest of ease. It was only later, when he was alone, that it occurred to him that he'd been doing most of the talking.

As for Claudia, she could talk and laugh for hours. But when you thought about it, she had managed to keep the conversation going without giving more than a minimum of personal information.

For example, it had taken until Saturday for him to figure out that Claudia was a first-year nursing student at the school attached to Haven Lake Medical Center.

At first, when Claudia had said that she was living at the house of Dr. Harroldson, who was on the hospital staff, Pres had assumed that the Harroldsons were relatives and Claudia was just in town for a vacation. Then, yesterday, when he'd innocently asked if Dr. Harroldson was her uncle, Claudia had broken up laughing.

"Dr. Harroldson? My uncle?" she giggled. "Whatever gave you a silly idea like that?"

"You mean he's not? Then why are you staying at his house?"

"To be near the hospital, of course," Claudia had said, as if it were the most obvious piece of information in the world. "You know, for a small hospital Haven Lake is really first rate. The nursing school is one of the best anywhere."

"Oh! You're studying nursing!" Suddenly, it all made sense to Pres. "But why didn't you tell me that last night?"

"Didn't I?" Claudia looked surprised, then smiled. "Maybe I didn't want to make a big deal out of it. Maybe I was worried that you wouldn't like hearing that I'm already out of high school. I'm only a couple of months older than you," she added. "I graduated from high school three months after my seventeenth birthday."

"But why aren't you living in the dorm?" Pres had asked.

"Well, y'know, the only rooms there are doubles

and triples. And I do like my privacy."

"I see," Pres had said. Even though he wasn't entirely sure he did see. Living miles away from the dorm, in the house of a middle-aged doctor and his wife, sounded a little too private to him. But then Claudia hardly had the personality of a hermit. Maybe she just wanted to be away from all the petty rules and regulations that went with dormitory life.

Though he would have been interested in meeting the Harroldsons, Pres didn't get a chance. Claudia was waiting for him on the porch of the house, and she bounded down the steps and jumped into the passenger seat of the Porsche almost before he'd had a chance to come to a full stop.

Her cheeks were pink from the cold, making Pres aware all over again of just how beautiful Claudia's complexion was. Her skin was almost translucent, fragile looking.

Which was the real Claudia? he found himself wondering. The assertive, self-confident girl she mostly seemed to be? Or the delicate southern belle she looked so much the picture of?

As they approached the Tilford house, Pres began to wonder if he ought to be nervous about the possibility of their running into his mother.

Mr. and Mrs. Tilford were going out to dinner that evening, so there would be no family meal at home, which was one reason he'd thought it would be a good opportunity to invite Claudia over to the house. They could snack on leftovers and use the den, a comfortable room with a fireplace and a terrific quadraphonic sound system, all without having to face the ordeal of a major interrogation from his folks.

Pres knew that his mother could be awfully formidable, even in a brief encounter. He could still remember the time that she had had one drink too many and embarrassed Kerry half to death with some offhand remark about the "floosies" her son brought home. Knowing his mother as he did, Pres had known that the remark wasn't directed at Kerry personally. But he'd never quite been able to convince Kerry of that. She'd been nervous around his house from that time on.

Maybe if I'm lucky, Pres told himself, when we arrive Mom will have already left to meet Dad. At the very least, maybe she'll be in her room getting dressed, so that I won't have time for more than a flying introduction on her way out.

But he couldn't be lucky every day.

When they had pulled the car to a stop in the long semicircular driveway and made their way into the foyer, Pres saw that his mother was already dressed and seated in the living room. There was no way that he could postpone the inevitable meeting.

Claudia slipped off her coat, revealing that she was dressed as casually as possible in a pair of bleached-out; skintight jeans; a slightly frayed cotton turtleneck; and a colorful, hand-knit vest. Yet somehow, in spite of everything, she looked incredibly elegant. The boots she had on were well worn but had obviously been very expensive when new. And around her neck was a chain of very thin, handcrafted silver links. Pres had never seen anything quite like it. Like Claudia herself, it was special and different and faintly exotic.

Pres looked up from admiring the necklace to find his mother descending on them with the determination of a Coast Guard cutter under full steam.

"Why, isn't this nice!" Felicia Tilford crooned. "Just think, if I'd left a few minutes earlier I would have missed meeting your little friend. Now we'll have a chance to get acquainted!"

Pres felt his stomach begin tying itself into little knots, but Claudia looked undismayed. "You must be Miz Tilford," she drawled, adding a few extra layers of southerness to her usual soft accent. "What a charming house you have!

"And look at these *interesting* portraits," she added, zeroing in on the gallery of Tilford ancestors that lined the foyer. "Why, they must be heirlooms! You'll have to tell me all about their subjects!"

Mrs. Tilford was not used to having her house, the largest in Tarenton, described as merely "charming." And she was even less used to dealing with people who refused to allow her to dominate the flow of conversation.

Gamely, she managed to steer the talk away from the portraits and shepherd Claudia and Pres into the living room.

"Virginia is horse country, isn't it?" Mrs. Tilford said. "You look like a horsewoman to me. I wish you'd teach my son. The only exercise he

65

gets is prancing around with that pack of cheer-leaders at his school. Riding would be much more . . . appropriate."

"Sorry to disappoint you, Mrs. Tilford," Claudia said. "But I don't know a *thing* about horses. I'm afraid I avoid exercise at all costs. It's so boring."

Pres noticed that his mother's eyes were fastened on Claudia's well-worn boots. Riding boots. It occurred to him that for some reason he couldn't figure out, Claudia was lying. She always used that "it's-so-boring" line when she wanted to avoid talking about something.

"My son tells me you're studying nursing," his mother said, changing the subject. "It's a wonderful profession, I think," Mrs. Tilford said.

Then she frowned. "It's such a shame that nowadays the really bright, ambitious girls all want to be doctors."

Pres cringed. Sometimes he wondered how his mother managed it. For one who put a premium on "gracious" conversation, she seemed to have an unerring instinct for insulting people.

Claudia, however, seemed unbothered. "I don't know about bright," she said, "but no one has ever accused me of being ambitious. I think all this talk about the importance of delayed gratification is overrated, don't you, Miz Tilford? I mean, what's the point of being young if you can't find time to enjoy yourself?"

Felicia Tilford looked as if she were ready to change the subject again. "I suppose so, dear," she said weakly. "But tell me, what made you decide to go into nursing?"

"Why, I never actually decided," Claudia said, sounding a bit surprised. "You know, sometimes things just seem to fall into place."

After that, the discussion settled down a bit. Mrs. Tilford started telling a story about how when she was a volunteer at the hospital she had practically fainted the first time she had seen blood. Claudia laughed sympathetically. Pres felt his attention fading in and out, as the conversation went on.

"I've got to hand it to you," he said when his mother had finally gone and left them alone. "A lot of people find my mom a little bit off-putting. You handled her just fine."

"She's not so bad," Claudia said. "Anyway, it's not as if I were auditioning to become part of the family. I admit that if I had serious designs on you, I might be just a little bit scared of your mother."

Pres wasn't sure whether he liked this or not. Obviously, he wasn't eager for Claudia to have "designs" on him, as she put it. But he wasn't sure he liked the fact that she seemed to consider such a thing totally unthinkable.

I must be losing my mind, Pres told himself. The last thing I want is a long-term relationship. I ought to be thrilled to find a girl who's just as independent as I am. So why do I feel a little bit hurt?

After fixing themselves a platter of fruit, cheese,

and crackers from the well-stocked kitchen, the two of them settled down in the den and started looking through the record collection.

"I have a confession to make," Pres said. "Listening to you talk to my mom, I started to feel kind of guilty that I haven't asked you more about your classes and training and so on. But the truth is, I guess I'm just allergic to the whole subject of sickness and hospitals. It's all so depressing and . . . I don't know, creepy."

"No problem," said Claudia, who was busy selecting a Billie Holiday album from a pile of old jazz vocalists. "Hospitals and sickness are the last things in the world I want to think about when I'm with you, Pres."

She put the record onto the turntable very carefully and flicked the automatic play switch.

"Hey, Claudia," he said. "How come you told my mother you don't ride? Those are riding boots you're wearing. She wasn't going to force you to take me out and teach me or anything."

"I know," she said. "I just didn't want to discuss it."

"Why not? What's the big mystery?"

Claudia removed the clip that she'd been wearing in her ponytail and shook her hair so that it fell in a cascade over her shoulders. It was a small gesture, but Pres thought it was about the sexiest thing he'd ever seen. "What's wrong with a little mystery?" she said, laughing.

"Nothing, I guess," Pres admitted. "It's just that sometimes I feel as if I don't know you at all. Maybe we should talk more."

She stopped examining the stereo set and crossed the room to snuggle down beside him on the big glove-leather couch. "That would be a terrible waste of time, when there are so many better things we could be doing."

CHAPTER

"Wouldn't it be great not to have to think about how much things cost for once?" Mary Ellen Kirkwood sighed.

She was standing in front of the supermarket's gourmet counter, surveying the shelves crammed full of expensive luxury foods. Fancy jams. Pâtés. Refrigerated tins of beluga caviar. Imported escargots packaged complete with the empty snail shells for restuffing and a set of silver-plated tongs.

Mary Ellen's younger sister Gemma was less than impressed. "Yuck!" she said. "Who would want to eat that junk, anyway? Snails! And black, gooey fish eggs! It's disgusting. Don't tell me you'd actually try that stuff."

Mary Ellen sighed and pushed her overloaded supermarket cart farther down the aisle. "That's not the point," she tried to explain. "It's just that I'd like to be able to have the choice."

She pointed toward the cart. "Look at this! Everything we get has to be the cheapest of its kind in the store. Doesn't that get to you sometimes?"

Gemma surveyed the cart, which was filled with giant economy sizes and special sale items and generic brand canned goods and ketchup. Actually, she was rather proud of her ability to find bargains and compute which brands were the least expensive. It was obvious from her expression that she didn't share Mary Ellen's disgust with the whole project. "I don't know," she said doubtfully. "We get along okay."

"Sure," said Mary Ellen. "But I'd like to do more than just get along. Doesn't it ever bother you that we can't buy really nice things? The supermarket isn't so bad, but what I really hate is when Mom insists on buying underwear and stuff like that at the five and ten. Just because they have the lowest prices.

"You know what?" she went on. "As soon as I get my first real modeling assignment, the first thing I'm going to do is go to the fanciest department store in New York and stock up on lace-trimmed slips and satin teddies. I'll buy whole shopping bags full of expensive lingerie. All of it one hundred percent silk and satin. In fact, just wait till you come visit me. You won't find an ounce of polyester in my whole apartment!"

"That will be neat," said Gemma, homing in on the only part of Mary Ellen's fantasy that interested her. "Can I really come visit you in New York? All by myself?"

"Sure. Maybe you could even get a job there. Or you could live with me and go to school. How about that?"

Gemma frowned. "I don't think so. I'm not sure I'd want to be so far away from home."

Sometimes Mary Ellen found it hard to believe that she and her sister could be so unalike. Getting away from home was the thing she wanted most in the world. She loved her family, but she hated the way they lived. She hated having to count every penny, and she hated the tackiness of her home, from the garish turquoise color it was painted to the cheap ceramic figurines and artificial flowers that her mother plunked down in every spare inch of available space inside.

Mrs. Kirkwood's idea of decorating was that, since she couldn't afford quality, she would settle for quantity. Having lots of knickknacks around, she liked to say, "brightens things up."

Gemma, oblivious to Mary Ellen's train of thought, had just had a brainstorm of her own. "Maybe Mom and Dad will win the lottery," she suggested. "Then you won't have to leave home and be a model after all. We'd have all the money we could spend, and we'd still be together."

"Fat chance," Mary Ellen said.

If it weren't so hopeless, she would have tried to explain to Gemma why winning the lottery wouldn't make a bit of difference. Though she talked a lot about wanting to be rich, having money was really just the tip of the iceberg, when it came to her daydreams. She wanted to try to succeed in a big-time career. To see different parts of the country. Of the world. To have all kinds of exciting experiences. Even if her family had as much money as the Tilfords, she would never be satisfied hanging around Tarenton all her life.

Unfortunately, it was all but impossible to try to tell Gemma these things. Except for Mary Ellen, the Kirkwood family seemed to consider ambition to be a variety of adolescent disease that she would soon grow out of, just as she had outgrown her baby plumpness.

"Just wait," her father had said only last night. "You'll give up these fancy ideas of yours soon enough. Once you start thinking about marriage and a family, all that other stuff starts to seem pretty remote."

Maybe Dad was right, for that matter.

And that, Mary Ellen told herself, was exactly why she wasn't going to let herself get trapped into a situation where she might start thinking along those lines. That was why, above all, she wanted to avoid getting caught up in a romance with Patrick Henley — the one boy in town who made the word *forever* start to dance around in front of her eyes.

Mary Ellen tore off the bottom section of her long shopping list and handed it to Gemma. "Here," she said, "you get these things and we'll get finished faster. Mom's probably waiting for us in the parking lot already."

After Gemma tore off in the general direction of the bakery aisle, Mary Ellen decided to entertain herself by pretending that there was a team of TV producers in the store, looking for typical shoppers to star in one of those consumer-testimonial type of ads.

If there *were* such people around, would they be likely to pick Mary Ellen Kirkwood out of the crowd?

Mary Ellen had no doubts about her looks. She had the kind of blonde, blue-eyed beauty that is always in style. But sometimes she wondered if her personality was outgoing enough. In spite of being captain of the cheerleading squad, she knew in her heart that she wasn't really the friendly, outgoing type. Not the way Angie Poletti was, for example. She had too many fierce ambitions and conflicting desires for her to be as open and generous as Angie was.

Still preening for her imaginary producers, Mary Ellen forced a smile to her lips and checked the results in the reflecting glass door of a frozen food cabinet.

Suddenly, she frowned again. What a dull, boring fantasy!

Daydreams are free, she lectured herself sternly. If you're going to daydream, why not at least think up something more exciting for yourself than a role in some commercial for a detergent or a headache medicine?

Why couldn't she be more like Walt, for instance? In appearance, Walt was just about the least romantic-looking guy in their class, at least from Mary Ellen's point of view. His chunky body and round face had "good kid" written all over them. But in his imagination, Walt was always acting out elaborate fantasies of himself as a detective, or a spy, or undercover agent. No matter how down-to-earth the reality of his life might be, Walt had an image of himself as the outlaw type.

Outlaw! The thought brought Mary Ellen up short. She knew that there were not many kids besides herself who knew about Walt's secret fantasy life. She only knew herself because she and Walt had gotten into a discussion about it back when Vanessa was spreading the rumor that Mary Ellen was a shoplifter.

Walt had been one of the first to defend Mary Ellen against the false accusation, pointing out to whomever would listen that just being short of money didn't make someone more likely to be a thief.

She could still remember what Walt had said to her: "People don't steal just because they don't have money," he'd theorized back then. "Or even because they want things they can't afford. I bet nine times out of ten, stealing has nothing to do with material gain. People steal because they want to get away with something. To live out their fantasies."

Not being tempted to steal herself, Mary Ellen wasn't sure if this was true or not. But she couldn't help wondering whether Walt had been speaking from his own experience. There wasn't a single practical reason why Walt would have broken in to Tatum's jewelry store.

Unless . . . it just happened to be part of some crazy outlaw scenario that had gotten out of hand.

Deep in thought, Mary Ellen turned the corner and headed up the next aisle.

She looked up from her reverie just in time to see a madman bearing down in her direction, bent over one of the oversized grocery carts and riding it at top speed as if it were huge skateboard or a landbound surfboard.

"Look out!" she shrieked.

The crazy man pulled his cart up into a half wheelie and brought it to a sudden halt, just inches before it crashed into her. Then he stood up to his full height and flashed a big smile, showing off the most perfect set of teeth in Tarenton High.

"Patrick Henley!" she said. "I should have known it would be you."

Patrick was totally unabashed. "Well, if you're not surprised," he said, "at least tell me you're pleased to see me."

"Don't be silly," she said. Though if the truth were told, she was happy. As much as she tried to avoid getting involved with Patrick, every time she came face-to-face with him something inside her melted a little.

"I thought it was time that we discussed our date," he said. "Remember, we've only got five days left."

"I haven't the faintest idea what you're talking about," she lied.

"Then let me refresh your memory. We had a

bet. And you lost. So, as a result, you owe me one date. Any day this week."

Mary Ellen tried to look disgusted. "You're not going to hold me to that! What do you think I am? I don't sell dates, and I don't gamble them away either. It isn't right. It isn't . . . dignified."

Patrick grinned broadly. "But you did agree to the bet. Tell you what, Mary Ellen. If you keep your promise and go out with me, the world need never know how low you sank. If you fink out, I can't promise it won't be all over school."

"Okay, okay. When?"

"No better time than tonight," he suggested. "We could catch a movie right here at the mall. There's this movie about a pair of actresses who are really high-class jewel thieves. It's filmed in Europe and has all these decadent fashions and backgrounds, they say. Sounds like you'd love it."

"Jewel thieves! Ouch!" Mary Ellen exclaimed, remembering Walt again. "Some timing! A movie like that just would happen to be playing this week of all times."

Unless, possibly, it wasn't all coincidence. "You don't think that's how the thief got his inspiration, do you?" she asked Patrick, not daring to mention her suspicion that the thief was Walt after all.

Patrick shrugged. "I doubt it. Considering that the same movie is probably playing in half the theaters in the country."

"Yeah," she shot back, "but in half the towns in the country, the current movie is not necessarily the most inspiring thing going on. In wild and crazy Tarenton, it just about is."

"I couldn't have said it better myself," Patrick agreed. "So how about going with me tonight?"

Mary Ellen checked her watch. "I don't see how I can," she said. "Mom's probably waiting outside right now. I've got to finish the shopping and find Gemma. And then get all this stuff checked out and paid for."

"I'll help," Patrick volunteered. "If your mother doesn't mind, you can go on to the movie with me, and I'll still get you home pretty early."

Mary Ellen considered. Actually, she would like nothing better than spending the next few hours with Patrick. And a week night date was relatively safe. It would be understood from the beginning that she had to get home early . . . so she wouldn't be tempted to forget that she was determined not to get too involved.

"Okay," she agreed. "Here, just help me with these last few items."

She hefted a colossal-size jug of detergent from the shelf next to her and dumped it into Patrick's hands. Unexpectedly, he grimaced and pulled back his left hand, letting the jug go crashing to the floor.

Fortunately, it just skittered harmlessly down the aisle. But from the look on Patrick's face he was in real pain.

"I'm sorry," Mary Ellen said. "What did I do? Did I hurt you?"

Patrick shook his hand tentatively. "It isn't your fault. I guess I sprained my wrist Friday night. That's what I get for showing off on the diving board. It's been a little sore, so I skipped work the last few days."

Mary Ellen knew right away that Patrick's wrist must be more than just a little sore. Patrick worked weekends and after school on the truck he owned that was part of his father's private garbage collection company. The job brought him no end of razzing around school, and it embarrassed Mary Ellen to like a guy who spent most of his spare time elbow-deep in garbage. But one thing you had to say for Patrick, he was a conscientious worker. He wouldn't have taken several days off unless his wrist really hurt him.

"Let me see that," she said, taking a closer look.

Patrick's wrist was still obviously swollen, and the skin had begun to turn a nauseating greenish-blue color.

"Shouldn't you have a bandage or a cast on that?" Mary Ellen asked. "What did the doctor say?"

"I don't need a doctor," Patrick said too quickly. "It'll be fine in a few days."

"But it could be broken!"

It was useless arguing with Patrick once he had decided to go into his stubborn mode. Mary Ellen let him tag along while she and Gemma finished their errand and paid at the checkout counter. Once her mother got a look at Patrick's wrist, Mary Ellen knew she'd have an ally.

Sure enough, when they got the groceries out

to the Kirkwoods' station wagon, Patrick drew Mrs. Kirkwood's attention by trying to help load the bags with his one good arm.

"What's the matter? What did you do to your wrist?" Mary Ellen's mother demanded.

"He hurt it on Friday night," Mary Ellen said immediately. "And he still hasn't had it checked by a doctor."

Mrs. Kirkwood gave Patrick a solid thump between his shoulder blades. "Get in the car, young man. We're going to drop you at the emergency room right now. You've got to have that x-rayed."

Patrick looked startled. Big and burly, with a reputation as a hell-raiser, he wasn't used to being talked to as if he were five years old and too dumb to know his own mind. For a minute, he looked as if he might just walk away. Then he relented. "Yes, ma'am," he said, and crawled into the backseat a bit sheepishly.

"I'm afraid we can't wait for you in the emergency room," Mrs. Kirkwood explained as she drove. "I've got dinner to fix. Not to mention lots of frozen food that will spoil if I don't get it back home soon. Can someone in your family pick you up when you're finished?"

"No problem," said Patrick.

Mary Ellen could see now from the expression on Patrick's face that he really was in pain. Probably he'd been hurting for days, and just put on a big act to deny even to himself how bad the wrist was.

She felt a wave of sympathy washing over her. For once, instead of acting tough and cocky, Patrick seemed vulnerable. He needed her, and she wanted to be there at his side to offer moral support.

She reached over and gently stroked the back of his head. "Maybe I'd better stay with you in the emergency room," she said. "I don't mind missing dinner."

Patrick looked grateful.

Then suspicious.

"I suppose this will count as our date," he said. "And me in agony and with one arm out of commission!"

Mary Ellen wanted to scream. Here she was, trying to reach out to Patrick for once, to be warm and sympathetic — and all he could think about was their stupid date! At times like this she wondered if Patrick really cared about her as a person at all. Or was he just completely caught up in the game of pursuing her?

"Forget I offered," she said, squirming back over toward her side of the backseat.

"What's wrong? What did I do now?" Patrick said, stunned.

"I said forget it," Mary Ellen repeated.

Fortunately, at that moment they pulled into the emergency ward driveway. "I don't have all night," Mrs. Kirkwood said impatiently. "Stay or come with us, Mary Ellen. Make up your mind. But do it now."

"I don't need a nursemaid," Patrick said

huffily. "If I have to be on my way to the hospital to get a kind word from you, then I guess I can do without. Forget it."

Making up Mary Ellen's mind for her, he bounded out of the car and strode into the hospital alone.

CHAPTER

8

Mary Ellen Kirkwood wasn't the only person in town who'd noticed the coincidence that a jewel-theft movie happened to be playing at the mall.

Vanessa Barlow, disgusted that she couldn't get her father to take any interest in suspending Walt and Nancy from the cheerleading squad, had decided to spend the early part of the evening at the Pinelands Mall Theater. She had talked Evie Caird into going with her.

Originally, the plan had been to see a rock music spoof called *Culture Crumbs*. But as soon as Vanessa saw what was playing in the theater's second screening room, her mind latched onto the possibilities. "Come on, Evie," she said, in the tone of a general issuing an order to the troops. "We've just changed our minds about what movie we're going to see."

"But I want to see *Culture Crumbs*!" Evie protested. "The only reason I came with you in the first place is because tomorrow is the last night it will be playing."

"So go tomorrow," Vanessa said, unmoved. "There's something important about this movie that I want you to see."

Half an hour into the feature, Evie still had no idea what was so important about *Command Performance*, a film about a troupe of actors who are rehearsing to perform for the Queen of England, and at the same time plotting to steal the crown jewels from the Tower of London. The movie wasn't bad; it just happened not to be the one that Evie was interested in. "Why are we here?" she whispered to Vanessa. "What's the big deal?"

"Don't you get it?" Vanessa hissed back. "It's about a jewel theft. This is where our friendly neighborhood thief got his inspiration."

Evie let out a croak of laughter that set heads turning all over the theater. "From the crown jewels to the Tatum's display window! Only you could see a connection!"

"Look again!" Vanessa commanded.

On the screen, the male lead, who was also the propman in the theater company and the sidekick of the two actress-thieves, was leading a pair of detectives in a wild car chase through the streets of London. The character was played by a short, thick-set actor. And he drove a black jeep, not unlike Walt Manners'.

"I see what you mean," Evie acknowledged

reluctantly when the movie was over and the lights had come up in the theater. "But so what? It's just a coincidence. It doesn't mean Walt is a thief. If you believe that, then Nancy is lying, too. And so is the manager of the Pizza Palace."

Vanessa made a face. People who insisted on talking about facts all the time were so boring.

"If Walt isn't a thief, then he should be," she said illogically. "Why should a clown like him get to be a cheerleader when I'm not? And Nancy is just as bad, pretending to be so sweet when she really isn't."

On the way out of the theater, Vanessa stopped to check her appearance in the reflection of the glass coming-attractions case. She pulled her long black hair back from her face experimentally and checked her profile. "Don't you think I look a little bit like that actress in the picture?" she asked Evie. "The brunette?"

"Not really," Evie said. She was feeling too sulky over missing the movie she'd wanted to see to waste energy on flattering Vanessa. It almost didn't matter since Vanessa ignored her anyway.

"I think it might be fun to be a glamorous international criminal," Vanessa mused, mostly to herself. "Unfortunately, there isn't anything around Tarenton worth taking."

Except other girls' boyfriends, Vanessa thought. And that gave her an idea for how she might be able to profit from Nancy Goldstein's troubles after all.

* * *

Patrick Henley, meanwhile, was still in the emergency ward at Haven Lake Medical Center. The evening he'd hoped to spend with Mary Ellen was turning into a big bore.

He had already been waiting to see a doctor for nearly two hours and there were still several people ahead of him. The nurse, a gray-haired woman called Mrs. McGonigle, was not sympathetic. "You waited four days to show up here," she pointed out when Patrick complained. "You're not going to convince me now that you're a desperate case. So you'll just have to wait until the real emergencies are taken care of."

Some of the people ahead of him did not strike Patrick as real emergencies either. There was a little boy who had stuck a bean up his nose, and who seemed less upset about the problem than his mother, who was practically hysterical. And there was an elderly man who complained that he was picking up Kansas City Athletics games on his hearing aid receiver. Patrick tried to explain to him that this was impossible. For one thing, baseball season hadn't started. For another, there hadn't been a team called the Kansas City Athletics for years.

"They're called the Royals now," he told the man.

This news did not appear to make any great impression. "That's what's so darned annoying," the man said. "Darned annoying."

Giving up, Patrick settled back in his chair and flipped through some old magazines. Unfortunately, at least half of the models in the advertisements were blonde and lithe and reminded him, in an unsettling way, of Mary Ellen. If he hadn't been so hotheaded, she would be sitting beside him right this minute, holding his hand — his healthy one — and smothering him with sympathy.

In his heart, he believed that fate intended him and Mary Ellen to end up together. It was a good thing, too, because otherwise he would have become completely discouraged long before this. Mary Ellen saw his love as a trap that could keep her from ever fulfilling her ambitions of getting out of Tarenton and becoming a high-fashion model. And on the rare occasions when she relented and treated him nicely, he usually managed to mess things up.

It was just that he was so crazy about her that he could never let well enough alone. If she agreed to go out with him one night, he immediately started badgering her about the next. And so on. What he really wanted was to sweep Mary Ellen off her feet, carry her to the nearest church, and marry her. And she knew it, too. Some girls might have liked the idea, or at least found it flattering. Mary Ellen, on the other hand, was so turned off by the prospect of marriage that she looked like she wanted to run for her life whenever the thought so much as crossed his mind.

He had often thought that Mary Ellen's reaction to him might be completely different if he didn't come from the family that owned Henley Trash. Slinging garbage was not exactly a glamorous occupation, and he knew all too well how Mary Ellen must see him. Big and boisterous and over-eager. A little too loud. And with quite a few too many rough edges. If only his name were Tilford instead of Henley, he might have a chance.

While Patrick was mulling over the Mary Ellen problem, a tall, slender brunette in jeans; high, well-scuffed boots; and a black cotton turtleneck came running into the reception area. "Hi, Katie," she said, greeting Mrs. McGonigle. I hope I'm not late. I was supposed to meet Dr. Harroldson at ten to go over this morning's X rays, but I forgot to tell my date that I had to be back early."

Late or not, it was easy to see that Mrs. McGonigle was very fond of the girl. "Don't you worry about that," she reassured her. "He's still upstairs. We're behind schedule as usual, what with so many people deciding to have emergencies."

Half an hour or so later, Patrick's turn came at last.

"I'm going to have to take you up to x-ray myself since we're shorthanded," Mrs. McGonigle announced, sounding none too pleased. She pointed to an empty wheelchair resting against the wall. "Sit," she ordered him.

"It's my wrist that's hurt, not my leg," Patrick protested. "Why can't I just walk up there under my own steam?"

"Because the hospital's insurance company doesn't trust you to get there without breaking your leg on the way." She sized up Patrick with a knowing squint. "In your case, they're probably right. You look like the accident-prone type to me."

Patrick laughed. "All too true, I'm afraid."

Naturally, when they got to the X-ray department there was another wait. In one of the offices separated from them by a glass partition, Patrick could see the girl who had just spoken to Mrs. McGonigle downstairs, having an earnest talk with a middle-aged, white-coated doctor. He had thought the girl looked familiar when he first saw her. Now he was sure of it.

"What's that girl's name?" he asked Mrs. McGonigle. "I know I've seen her around somewhere. I just can't figure out where."

"Claudia Randall," Mrs. McGonigle said. "A sad case, that one."

"Really?" Patrick found this hard to believe. "She certainly doesn't look sick to me."

"Poor dear," Mrs. McGonigle sniffed. "She was a champion horsewoman. Then she had this horrible accident. Got thrown and hurt her back something awful. She's walking now, but she may not be for long. Dreadful for a young girl like that to have to think about being paralyzed."

"But why? What's wrong?"

"I can't tell you that," the nurse snapped, suddenly aware that she had given out confidential information. "I've said too much already."

They still weren't ready to x-ray Patrick's wrist. Mrs. McGonigle got bored waiting around and wandered off down the hall. Patrick continued to study the face of the brunette in the office. She had very long hair, fine and straight. Her face wasn't beautiful exactly, not in the way that Mary Ellen's was, at least. But she was striking. He was sure he'd seen her before.

"It's stuffy in here," the doctor with her said. He'd gotten up and opened the door to the office cubicle. Obviously, he didn't know that there was anyone in the outer waiting room.

Patrick felt torn. He knew he ought to cough or make a noise or say something to warn the pair in the office that he could now overhear their conversation. But at the same time, he was curious. Eavesdropping wasn't his style. Still, just this once he decided to make an exception.

"Forget it," the girl, Claudia, was saying. "I don't want to go to California. And I don't want to have an operation."

"But it's crucial," the doctor said gravely. "We've been over this before. The bone fragment is lodged near your spine. If you don't have it removed, it's likely to shift position sooner or later. You could be paralyzed for life."

"And if I do have it, the operation might not work anyway. I could be paralyzed even sooner. Or I could die."

Dr. Harroldson looked pained. "I won't lie to you. There is some risk. But I wouldn't recommend this course of action if I didn't think the risk was a lot less than doing nothing."

"Some risk!" Claudia said sarcastically "That's easy for you to say. No, thank you. I'd rather enjoy life and take my chances. No one's going to get me back in a hospital bed voluntarily."

The girl waved an accusing finger at the doctor. "I thought you asked me to come up north and stay with your family because you were my parents' friend. But you're just like all the rest of them. All you want is to talk me into changing my mind."

"Claudia, I can understand that you're afraid. Fear is a natural reaction. . . ."

"I've told you a million times," she shot back, "fear has nothing to do with it!"

Of course it does, Patrick thought. He could tell by the tremor in the girl's voice that she was scared to death. And no wonder!

Claudia got to her feet as the doctor snapped off the illuminated screen where her X rays had been displayed. They were preparing to leave. Patrick quickly turned his chair to face the wall, hoping they'd think he'd been dozing or was too out of it to pay attention to their discussion.

It was all wasted effort. Neither Claudia nor Dr. Harroldson paid the slightest bit of attention to him on their way out. They were too worried about their own problems to care.

After what seemed like an eternity, Mrs. McGonigle returned with the news that the X-ray technicians were finally ready for him. Two young men took several X-ray views of his wrist, and sometime later a young resident came out and informed him that he had sprained some ligaments.

"You're lucky," she said. "You won't need a

cast. But you will have to have your wrist bandaged for a week or two. And of course, you won't be able to do anything that puts pressure on it for a while. I hope you're not left-handed."

"Nope," Patrick said morosely.

With expert speed, the intern placed a foam rubber and plastic support on the inside of his wrist, extending up into the palm of his hand, then bandaged around it.

Patrick thought of protesting. How was he supposed to work with his left hand immobilized? How was he going to drive his truck? The wrist would probably have been fine in a few days, just left to heal by itself. He hated all this fuss. Why did Mary Ellen have to interfere, anyway? And why had he let her?

He wished he'd never come to the hospital. Never overheard that awful conversation between that girl, Claudia, and the doctor. He knew he should probably feel fortunate by comparison. He and Mary Ellen, as bad as their problems were at times, didn't have to face any really scary choices like that. They were lucky.

For some reason though, he just felt depressed. Instead of enjoying their good luck, the two of them spent most of their time avoiding each other. Or squabbling. Or generally making themselves miserable.

Maybe, he thought, being hung up on Mary Ellen was just a huge waste of time and energy. The only reason that he bothered at all was that the prospect of losing her forever seemed even more unthinkable.

CHAPTER

"It's true that nothing ever happens in Tarenton. But this is the place where it's all not happening."

Claudia laughed, and Pres felt rewarded, the way he always did when he managed to say something that amused her. He loved the clear, bell-like sound of her laughter. It was so feminine, so elegant, compared to the laughs of the other girls he'd known.

Getting out of the driver's seat of the Porsche, he went around to open Claudia's door for her. Even his manners had improved over the last few days. He knew that he and Claudia made a handsome couple together, and didn't want to do anything to spoil the effect. They were complimentary opposites: He, tall and broad-shouldered, with dark blond hair and a square-jawed, solid sort of good looks. And she, dark and fragile-looking, with her fine hair pulled back so that it hung straight down her back in a narrow, gleaming ribbon of black.

It was Wednesday evening, and it was a shame that they hadn't anywhere more romantic to go than the Pizza Palace. However, Claudia had been hinting strongly that she wanted to go somewhere where she could at least see other people their age. And what with the Pizza Palace being the talk of the town ever since last Friday, it was natural that she was curious about it.

Though he couldn't blame Claudia for wanting to be more social, Pres had no desire to introduce her to his friends. It was selfish of him, he knew, but he didn't want to share her. He wanted to have all her attention all the time they were together. He felt as if she belonged to a special, precious part of his life. And though he wasn't sure exactly what could go wrong, the idea of bringing Claudia together with his friends made him uneasy.

Fortunately, Claudia wasn't the only one who was curious about the Pizza Palace's recent publicity on Channel Eight. The place was busier than Pres had ever seen it on a week night. Paradoxically, it was easier to ignore the familiar faces in the crowd than it would have been if the restaurant had been half empty.

Pres led Claudia to a table for two in the rear part of the room that was usually reserved, by unspoken agreement, for older patrons and dating couples who didn't want to be disturbed. Seated where they were, it was a good deal less likely that any of the kids he knew would invite themselves to join his party for two.

As it happened, the arrival of Pres and Claudia caused no more than a passing flicker of interest.

Speculation about who Claudia might be was interrupted a few minutes later when Ben Adamson showed up, in the company of Hank Vreewright, formerly Tarenton's best basketball player, now on the sidelines due to a knee injury.

Stopping at the counter, Ben put in an order for a large pizza with a number of extras.

Johnny Junior, the manager's son who was working the counter that night, made Ben the same offer he'd been suggesting to patrons who ordered large pizzas all evening long. "Why don't you just take one with all the trimmings?" he said. "It's cheaper than ordering add-ons individually.

"We call it the Alibi Special," he added with a wink.

Johnny Junior had no idea that he was talking to Nancy Goldstein's steady boyfriend. Carried away by the Pizza Palace's mention on the local TV news, Johnny was intent on milking the humor of the situation for all it was worth. And then some. He'd probably made the same joke at least fifty times over the last few days.

Almost every single one of his customers could have told him that he'd just tried the joke once too often.

"That's not funny, buster," Ben growled. "If

95

I hear that you've made that crack once more, it'll be your face that needs some add-ons."

"It's my place, and I'll say whatever I want," Johnny Junior retorted. "You can't threaten me."

"I just did," Ben reminded him.

Johnny Junior hesitated. In spite of his name, he was twice the size of his father, with a shelf full of Golden Gloves trophies sitting at home. He could have taken on Ben and Hank together if he really wanted to. On the other hand, the last thing he wanted was to spoil a profitable evening by having a fight on the premises. There were certain kinds of publicity his restaurant didn't need.

Vanessa Barlow happened to be sitting with a group at one of the tables nearest the counter and, for once, she decided it was in her interest to play peacemaker.

"Forget it," she urged Ben, putting a conciliatory arm around his waist. "He didn't know you'd take it personally.

"It isn't *his* fault," she added, stressing the *his* in a way that made it clear she was placing the blame squarely on Walt and Nancy.

"Come on, Ben. Let's get out of here," Hank Vreewright put in. "She's right. It isn't worth making trouble over."

Ben looked around him as if he'd just awakened from a dream and found himself in the last place in the world he wanted to be. "I'm not hungry anymore," he told Hank. "You may as well stick around. There's no reason for you to leave just because I feel like it."

Hank, recognizing that he was being told in a polite way that Ben felt like being left alone, shrugged his shoulders and ambled off in the direction of a table full of seniors.

Vanessa, however, did not take a hint that easily. Ignoring the fact that Ben didn't seem to want her, she gave a determined shake of her thick mane of hair and followed him out into the parking lot.

"You know, you don't have to suffer in silence," Vanessa said, half running to keep up with Ben's long strides. "You could always cry on my shoulder."

Ben stopped and turned around, assessing the offer. In spite of the cold, Vanessa was wearing a sweater with a deep V neck. No two ways about it, Vanessa had a terrific figure and great skin that retained the tawny glow of summer even after months of north country winter. What's more, he ought to be grateful to her for stopping him from getting into a pointless, and probably painful, fight with Johnny Junior.

"It's a tempting offer," he acknowledged, "but I think I've got enough troubles right now. Even though Nancy and I are on the skids at the moment, I do intend to find a way to patch things up with her."

"It seems to me you've got some competition in that department," Vanessa suggested. "Walt was acting awfully protective of her the other day, or so I heard."

Ben refused to acknowledge that he was being needled. "Nancy isn't involved with Walt. Not that way," he said. "She told me so."

"Maybe not," Vanessa pressed on, "but she didn't mind using him to make you jealous, did she?"

That observation hit home.

"So how does all this concern you?" Ben asked.

"I just hate to see a nice guy like you get pushed around. Maybe you ought to give Nancy a dose of her own medicine. Then she'd know how you feel."

"Y'know, maybe you're right," Ben said. "I think that's exactly what I should do."

Vanessa glowed with triumph.

Ben leaned down and gave her a quick, glancing kiss on the top of her head.

"Thanks, Vanessa. You've given me a great idea. You're a real pal," he said. And he turned and hurried off in the direction of his car.

Vanessa watched him go, her face reddening with anger and amazement. She wasn't sure exactly what Ben had in mind, but she did know that she had just been dumped on. "Low life," she hissed viciously in the direction of Ben's departing back. "How dare you walk out on me!"

Mary Ellen and Patrick pulled into the parking lot just in time to see the denouement of the scene.

"Whew!" gasped Mary Ellen. "I wonder what that was all about."

"I don't know," Patrick said, "but Vanessa

looks mean enough to stomp bunnies at Easter time."

"Knowing her," Mary Ellen guessed, "she probably tried to put a move on Ben and got told off. Ben's really cagey, you know. He's got street smarts. I don't think Vanessa has the brains to be any match for him."

"Brains," observed Patrick, "have never been Vanessa's secret weapon."

"Then what *is* her secret weapon? That's what I'd like to know," Mary Ellen said. "I can't see what the attraction is."

"Only a girl would have to ask," Patrick replied. "In a word, it's lust."

"Patrick! Don't tell me you feel that way! That's disgusting!"

Normally, that little exchange would have provided enough spark to get the two of them into a major argument. And with luck, they would go on more or less directly to the more enjoyable kiss-and-make-up stage. Tonight, however, Patrick failed to rise to the bait.

"Forget I even said it," he said dully. "Let's not get off on that subject, okay?"

Instead of feeling relieved, Mary Ellen was growing more disappointed by the minute. Ever since she'd found out about Patrick's injured wrist she'd been feeling mellow and sympathetic toward him. She just didn't have the heart to give him a bad time. She had agreed to their date tonight almost eagerly.

And she'd made a point of not complaining

that their transportation was his Henley Trash truck. Even though the cab was clean and the back of the truck had been thoroughly hosed down and deodorized, Mary Ellen felt that going out on a date in a garbage truck was humiliating and she was working hard not to show it.

She had even sat extra close to Patrick on the drive over, without getting the impression that he noticed or enjoyed having her close. And that was definitely a first.

Just when she was feeling almost ready to forget her caution, and enjoy being close to Patrick for once, he seemed to have lost interest. Something was very wrong.

"Is your wrist hurting you?" she asked solicitously. "We don't have to hang around here you know. We could go somewhere and be alone, if you want."

Even this suggestion didn't catch Patrick's interest. He acted as if he didn't even see the implications. "That's okay," he said. "It doesn't hurt. I'm just feeling kind of down tonight."

I can see that, Mary Ellen thought. But why? She knew it was a selfish thought but she couldn't help feeling resentful. When she acted as if she wanted nothing to do with Patrick, he pursued her like a lovesick, relentless puppy dog. And now that she was trying her best to be nice, he made her feel unwanted.

Inside the Pizza Palace, Patrick stopped at the table where Hank Vreewright was sitting and they got a brief rundown on the scene between Ben and Johnny Junior. Mary Ellen listened halfheartedly, tugging at Patrick's sleeve gently when he seemed to be on the verge of sitting down with the group.

"There's a table for two near the back," she said. "We could talk better there."

"Okay, if you want," he said without much interest, as Mary Ellen maneuvered him toward the rear of the room.

Once they were alone, silence descended. Not the dreamy kind of silence they occasionally shared when there was nothing that needed to be said because they were so much on the same wave-length. This was different. It was the silence of two people who are in completely different moods and can't find a common ground.

Desperate for something to distract them, Mary Ellen directed Patrick's attention to the other side of the room where Pres and his date were seated. Totally absorbed in whatever they were talking about, they might have been the only two customers in the place for all they cared. It was obvious that they were getting along a whole lot better than Mary Ellen and Patrick.

"That must be Pres's new love," Mary Ellen said. "He told me he was dating someone from out of town. But I don't think he wants to share her with us yet. She's a first-year nursing student at the school that's attached to the Haven Lake Medical Center. And according to Pres, she's the girl of his dreams."

"No she isn't," Patrick said.

Mary Ellen blinked. "How do you know?" she asked resentfully. "I mean, I realize that we've

101

all heard Pres say that before. But maybe this time it's for real. From what little he told me, they seem to have a lot in common. And she looks like a nice person."

Patrick held up his good hand, palm outward, in a gesture of peace. "I didn't mean that," he said. "What I meant was, she isn't a nursing student."

"Why do you say that? Do you know her?" she asked suspiciously.

"Not exactly. But I saw her at the hospital Monday night. I knew she looked familiar, but I couldn't remember where I'd seen her. That's it, though. She's the girl Pres was hanging around with at the pool party. Come to think of it, they must have left together early in the evening. I didn't notice them later on."

"Who cares? Tell me why you think she isn't a student," Mary Ellen demanded.

"It's a depressing story," Patrick said. "Are you sure you want to know?"

"Of course I do."

Patrick explained what he'd overheard while he was waiting for his X rays. "Apparently Dr. Harroldson knew her folks, and he and his wife invited her to come live with them. But she's scared to have the operation she needs. And if she doesn't she could end up in a wheelchair for life. Can you imagine what that would be like?"

"Awful," Mary Ellen agreed. "I can see why Pres lied and said she was a nursing student, though. He's probably afraid that if people know the truth they'll act awkward and say something really dumb."

"Could be," Patrick said. "Or else, he doesn't know the truth himself."

"But that's impossible!" Mary Ellen gasped. "I mean, he's got to know. They've been seeing each other every day since they met."

The more he thought about it, the more certain Patrick felt that he'd guessed right. "From what I heard," he told Mary Ellen, "it seemed to me that Claudia doesn't want to admit even to herself what's going on. She's trying to pretend the whole situation doesn't even exist. And I know Pres. He has a thing about sickness and physical weakness. He could hardly stand to look at my wrist, even now that it's bandaged. And that's no big deal. I bet if he were crazy about a girl and knew she had a serious problem like that, he wouldn't be walking around looking as if he hadn't a care in the world. One way or another, we'd know something was bothering him."

"That's terrible." Mary Ellen glanced over in Pres's and Claudia's direction again, almost guiltily. "You know what this means, don't you?" she said. "Somebody's got to tell Pres the truth."

"Uh uh," said Patrick. "No way. Never interfere, that's my motto. It really isn't any of our business."

"But if Pres really cares about her, doesn't he have a right to know? Besides," Mary Ellen added, "it looks to me as if Claudia cares a lot about him, too. What if Pres is the only person in the world who can talk her into having that operation? If we don't tell him, he might not get the chance until it's too late."

Patrick and Mary Ellen exchanged looks of total confusion, their own problems for once completely forgotten.

"I don't know," Patrick said finally. "You could be right, Mary Ellen. But who's going to tell him? I wouldn't know what to say, for one thing."

"Me, either," she admitted. "What are we going to do?"

CHAPTER

Ben had driven directly from the Pizza Palace to a place at the far end of the mall where there was a phone booth that he could use without being overheard.

Vanessa had inspired him, even if not quite in the way she'd hoped. He looked through the local phone book to find the number he needed, and then dialed, reaching his party on the second ring.

"Hey, Olivia," he said. "It's Ben Adamson."

"Ben. Hi."

Olivia sounded puzzled and a bit suspicious, and for a second Ben felt sure that his plan would never work. He decided to give it a try anyway. "I figured you'd probably be on your own tonight," he began. "I guess you and Walt haven't made up yet. Right?"

"You guessed it," Olivia confirmed.

"So I was thinking," he went on, "that maybe you'd like to get out of the house. Y'know, we could take a little ride and have a slice of pizza, maybe."

"Pizza!" Olivia all but shrieked. "What is this? Some kind of sick joke? I never want to hear the word *pizza* again as long as I live. Much less eat any. I should think you'd feel the same way, Ben."

"Hold on a second," Ben said. "I know just how you feel. I'm right with you. But I was thinking about the old saying. You know, the one that goes, 'Don't get mad. Get even.' "

There was a pause on the other end of the line as Olivia let this sink in. "Go on," she said.

"So it occurred to me that if Walt and Nancy can buy a pizza and take it up to the Overlook, so can we. I mean, why not? It's a free country."

That's a terrible idea, Olivia thought. Ben's plan could only make a bad situation worse. Half the town was probably at the Pizza Palace tonight, and if she showed up there with Ben the other half — including Walt and Nancy — would be sure to know about it by midnight. Besides, she didn't even like Ben all that much. He was a little bit too clever and self-satisfied for her to trust completely.

Nothing would be accomplished by going along with this crazy idea. Except that both of them would get revenge.

She knew it was childish but she said, "Okay. Pick me up at my place in fifteen minutes."

Ben arrived right on schedule. Olivia pulled on

her down parka and threw her favorite rose-colored scarf around her neck for luck. She was pretty sure already that she'd made a mistake saying yes, but she wouldn't dare give Ben an excuse to think that she was a total coward.

Seated in the front seat of Ben's car, she felt even more out of place. Ben was over six foot and without a doubt the oldest looking senior at Tarenton High. She, especially when bundled up in her coat and scarf, didn't look nearly her age. Together, the two of them made a bizarre-looking couple.

No one could possibly believe that we're out on an actual date, Olivia told herself. It's too ridiculous. We're completely opposite types.

But she knew very well that people would take their showing up together at face value.

It was hard to decide which she feared most: starting a serious rumor that could backfire, or being laughed at.

"I don't know if I can go through with this," she told Ben as they pulled into the Pizza Palace parking lot.

"Too late for cold feet now," Ben answered, patting her on the knee as if she were a little kid. Even though this had been his idea, he seemed to recognize that they were an unlikely couple.

"Come on," he said, "just stick close to me. You don't have to say anything."

Olivia followed him inside, aware of the buzz that went through the big, crowded room as soon as they were recognized.

Johnny Junior, not at all pleased to see Ben for

the second time that evening, was glowering at them from behind the counter.

"I changed my mind," Ben told him. "No hard feelings, okay? We'll take one of those Alibi Specials after all."

And he added in a voice loud enough to carry through the room, "And make that to go. We're going to eat it up at the Overlook."

There was total silence for about ten seconds and then Hank Vreewright, Ben's buddy, cracked up laughing. Johnny Junior, who'd been regarding Ben suspiciously, started to laugh, too. As the reaction spread, giggles and a buzz of speculative remarks rose from table to table.

Olivia's cheeks were burning. She wanted to flee, but Ben had an unobtrusive but firm hold on her. Getting into an argument with him right there would only have made matters that much worse.

Oddly, the whole scene seemed to have the opposite effect on Ben. The longer they stood there waiting for their order, the more relaxed he seemed. Even happy. He even started making small talk as if they really were out on a date, asking Olivia how she liked cheerleading and if she wasn't scared to do some of the gymnastic tricks that were her specialty on the squad.

When their pizza was ready, Ben paid and led the way back outside, balancing the box on one uplifted hand, waiter-style.

"We did it!" Ben exulted as soon as they were safely outside the swinging doors. "Did you see the looks on everyone's faces? What a trip!"

He's enjoying this too much, Olivia thought warily. Ben fully intended to make up with Nancy eventually, at least if she turned out to be willing. But in the meantime, he was determined to salvage his hurt pride and enjoy doing it.

When they got to the car, Ben dumped the pizza box onto the backseat unceremoniously. "We made our point," Olivia said. "Let's just go home now."

"Do you *have* to be such a straight arrow?" he said, exasperated. "Don't you have any sense of fun?"

It was an accusation that never failed to touch Olivia's deepest fears about herself. She'd spent most of her childhood in hospitals, or being towed by her mother from one doctor's office to another. Until just a few years ago, she'd never had close friends her own age. So it was true that she felt she'd been deprived of chances to do wild, impulsive things. Above all, she didn't want to be seen as stiff and stodgy, the kind of person who was always the first to run home to mother when the real action began.

"We'll just drive up to the Overlook," Ben said. "I'm not going to attack you or anything. If you don't like it up there, we'll leave.

"You were pretty good back there," Ben added. "It wasn't easy to pull off that little scene in front of all those people. You're a better actress than I thought you'd be."

Olivia warmed to the compliment. Ben was so different from Walt. Not just physically, either. Walt was so comfortable to be around. Ben was dangerous. Exciting. He was obviously never so happy as when he was doing something unpredictable.

Ben reached over and turned on the car radio. Instead of returning his hand to the steering wheel, he placed it squarely on Olivia's knee. His hand seemed huge, his long, narrow fingers almost as long as Olivia's whole hand.

"You're really tiny," Ben said. "Are you sure you're not just a little kid disguised as a high school junior?" he teased.

"Of course not," Olivia said. To her this was not a joke. Sometimes that was exactly how she felt.

They had reached the Overlook. Ben pulled off the highway and brought his car to a fast stop. "Then prove it," he challenged her.

I just might do that, Olivia thought to herself.

She was aware of Ben's closeness, of his rough-hewn, hawklike face bending close to kiss her. This must be, she thought irrationally, exactly what it feels like to be a mouse pursued by a bird of prey.

In the background, the radio droned on, the music interrupted by a commentary from Ramblin' Rudy, a late-night disc jockey who liked to intersperse playing records with airing his opinions on the day's events.

"Talk about nerve," he was saying. "Did you catch the Mannerses' TV breakfast show this morning?" The Mannerses did a good ten minutes of complaining about how the press intrudes on the private lives of celebrities' families. . . ."

110

Olivia pulled away from Ben abruptly. "Cool it," she said. "I've got to hear this."

"Could it be," Rudy asked insinuatingly, "that the Mannerses' sudden concern has something to do with the fact that Channel Eight news recently reported that their son Walt had been questioned by police as a suspect in a jewelry store burglary? What I want to know is, what makes the Manners family think that it deserves special treatment? Should the media suppress news just to protect their feelings? Do five hours a week on local TV entitle them to special treatment? And who says the Mannerses are celebrities, anyway?"

"Apparently Ramblin' Rudy thinks so," Ben commented sourly, "or he wouldn't go on and on about them."

He reached over and switched off the radio. "Forget about that, Olivia. Who cares? Walt's parents are his problem."

Olivia pushed him away. "I'm sorry, Ben. You may be right, but the problem is, I do care. Our being together is a big mistake."

She was expecting to get an argument. Instead, Ben let her go and slumped down onto his own side of the car seat.

"You're right," he said. "The only thing we're proving is how hurt we both were by what happened. We'd both rather be here with someone else."

Although this was exactly the point that Olivia had been trying to make, she couldn't help feeling a little insulted to think that Ben had been picturing himself with Nancy all along. "Then

111

why did you insist on coming up here?" she protested.

Ben grimaced. "No insult intended. I just think you'd be a lot more fun as a partner in revenge than Vanessa Barlow."

The mere mention of Vanessa made them groan in unison. "How could I not guess that Vanessa had a part in putting you up to this?" Olivia said. "I bet she already knows we're together and is spreading the word all over town."

"There's one consolation," Ben suggested. "If people hear about it from Vanessa, they won't believe it."

While Ben was driving Olivia home, Walt was in his bedroom in the Mannerses' glass and cedar house in the woods. He had heard Ramblin' Rudy's comments, too, and was seething with anger.

In fact, he'd been angry ever since dinnertime, when his parents casually mentioned that they'd received a few calls from loyal fans supporting the comments they'd made that day.

This was the first he'd heard about what had happened.

"Don't you think," he had complained, "that you ought to at least consult me before you discuss things on the air that concern me?"

"We never mentioned your name," his mother had said in self-defense. "Besides, you know that our show is ad-lib. We don't know what we're going to talk about until we actually say it."

Walt had sputtered with anger and frustration.

112

"Didn't it occur to you that you were just helping to keep the whole subject alive? You were doing exactly the thing you were complaining about."

Walt's father seemed stunned. "I never thought about it that way," he admitted. "But then it's our family that we talk about on the air. We're used to inviting the public into our living room. We've been doing it for years."

"Well, in the future," Walt said, "count me out. Having TV personalities for parents is nothing but a big pain. I don't want any part of it."

With that, Walt had left the dinner table and stormed off to his own room.

Walt's room, built over his parents' broadcasting studio and isolated from the rest of the house, was Walt's private refuge. It was equipped with its own sound system that he'd salvaged from secondhand professional equipment discarded by the studio, and stuffed full of objects that Walt had accumulated during various stages of his life: his butterfly and stamp collections; old film posters, records, and tapes; car magazines.

There had been a time, not that long ago, when Walt had believed that he could be totally happy in the solitude of the room. He wouldn't have minded at all if the rest of the world had just disappeared and left him in peace. Lately, though, he hadn't found holing up there very comforting.

Something was missing: Olivia.

Painful as their misunderstandings could be, being without Olivia was even worse. It was ridiculous that Olivia could even suspect he would be cheating on her with Nancy. Over the last few

113

days, he'd been tempted a hundred times to make the first move to smooth over their quarrel.

But he was just so hurt that Olivia hadn't been more supportive of him. She *should* have trusted him more.

Ramblin' Rudy's snide remarks made Walt think all over again that maybe he ought to make the first move to patch up his differences with Olivia. After all, he was used to hearing his private family problems discussed in front of an audience of thousands. It had been part of his life ever since he was a kid, when his folks used to use all his embarrassing childhood experiences as material for their show. Everything from his forgetting his lines when he was cast as Christopher Columbus in the third-grade play, to his unrequited crush on his fifth grade teacher Mrs. Martin had been grist for their mill.

Awful as this public exposure could be at times, he'd learned that it was possible to survive. It was wrong of him, though, to expect Olivia to be as thick-skinned about it as he was. He could empathize with her how she felt that the whole state knew he'd been at the Overlook with Nancy.

He was debating whether or not to pick up the phone and dial the Evans house, when the phone rang right under his hand. He picked up the receiver eagerly. If Olivia were making the first move to call him, so much the better!

"Hello, Walt?"

The voice on the line, Walt realized with a

sinking heart, was not Olivia's. It was Vanessa Barlow's.

"You'll never guess what I just heard from Hank," Vanessa said eagerly. "He was at the Pizza Palace tonight, and guess who came in?"

"Hey, it wasn't me. You can be sure of that," Walt said. "I've sworn off the place for good."

"Of course it wasn't," Vanessa said, annoyed. "Why would I be calling you to tell you that *you* were there?"

"I've no idea," Walt said. "Why would you be calling me to tell me that *anyone* was there? I'm not interested in your gossip."

"If that's the way you feel about it," Vanessa said. "I was just doing you a favor. . . ."

"That'll be the day!"

"I just think you ought to know what's going on," Vanessa continued. "Even if you are just about the last person in town to find out. It was Olivia and Ben. And they told everyone that they were on their way up to the Overlook."

Contrary to what Ben had predicted, Walt did believe it. Even Vanessa wouldn't have the nerve to make up a story like that. If it weren't true, there were too many people who had been at the Pizza Palace who could make a liar out of her.

"It makes no difference to me. I don't care," he told Vanessa, angrily slamming down the phone. But of course, he did care. A lot. Here he'd been, thinking of Olivia so fondly. And at that very moment, she was probably up at the Overlook with Ben Adamson.

115

CHAPTER

"We've talked it over, Angie, and we've decided that you're the one who's going to have to straighten this mess out."

Angie Poletti felt cornered. Mary Ellen and Patrick had corralled her after Thursday afternoon cheerleading practice and told her the whole story of Pres's new girl friend, Claudia Randall. The two of them had already talked the situation over at length and decided that Pres had to be told. And they had also come to the conclusion that Angie was the one to do it.

"Why me?" Angie protested. "You've been closer to Pres than I ever was," she reminded Mary Ellen not entirely tactfully. "And you, Patrick, are a guy. Don't you think Pres would rather hear this from you than from a girl?"

"Pres doesn't trust me enough," Mary Ellen pointed out. "The minute he'd hear that I wanted to talk to him about some problem having to do with Claudia, he'd freeze up."

"And you know me," added Patrick. "I'm just not good at that kind of thing. I'd be sure to put my foot in my mouth before I got halfway started. You're the sympathetic one. The sisterly type. People trust you."

"Forget it," Angie said, shaking her head. "I agree that someone should talk to Pres. Claudia needs help and he's in a position to help her. But it's up to you guys to do it. I'm tired of being the sisterly type. I don't want to be Tarenton High's answer to Dear Abby, either."

"But if you don't help us, Claudia may never have that operation," Mary Ellen protested. "She could end up spending the rest of her life in a wheelchair."

Guilt. Angie put her hands over her ears and tried not to listen. *Why am I such an easy mark for guilt trips?* she asked herself.

"Stop it, you guys," she said aloud. "I can't take it anymore."

"Does that mean that you'll talk to Pres?" Patrick asked.

"I'll think about it," she said. "I'll think about it. I mean, if the opportunity came up, and I had a chance to talk to Pres in confidence, I'd probably try. But I still don't think it's my problem. You two are the ones who ought to do it."

"Hey, thanks, Angie," said Patrick, thumping her on the back. "I knew we could count on you."

With a sinking heart, Angie ran outside, just

in time to catch the late school bus. This was the bus that picked up students who stayed for the after-school activity period and, as usual, it was less than half filled, mostly with underclassmen who were too young to drive or have friends who did.

Normally, she made it a point to be friendly to the younger kids on the bus. Coach Engborg was always reminding them that as cheerleaders they were leaders of the whole school, not just the little group of seniors who happened to be their friends. "Remember," the coach liked to say, "you're wearing that uniform on behalf of everyone." Angie kept the advice in mind, though she probably needed it less than anyone on the squad. She was just naturally outgoing and friendly.

Today, though, she was in no mood for freshman chatter. Glumly, she made her way to an empty seat at the rear of the bus and plunked herself down. Patrick and Mary Ellen certainly did have her number! The last thing she wanted was to get involved in Pres's love life! Her own — or rather her lack of one — was a problem that needed all her attention. But now that she knew the whole story, she was going to start feeling personally responsible. And if something happened to that girl, Claudia, before she talked to Pres, she'd never forgive herself.

Angie looked up just in time to see that the bus was passing the little convenience store at the foot of Cedar Point Road. And there, parked in front, was Pres's sports car. It's like a sign, Angie

118

thought. Something is telling me that I can't pass up this chance.

Shouting for the bus driver to stop, she grabbed her belongings and rushed out the door into the biting cold air.

Pres was inside, drinking a can of cola at the tiny counter in the rear of the store. "Hey, Angie," he said, "why don't you join me? I just stopped in to pick up some toothpaste and stuff on my way from practice, and I was so thirsty that I couldn't wait to get home."

Angie sat down on the stool next to Pres. Coach Engborg had been on a fitness kick all week long and had been working the squad pretty hard. But the real reason for the dry feeling in Angie's throat was that she was nervous about what she had to say to Pres.

"I've got to tell you something," she said to him, taking a deep breath. "Promise me you won't be mad, okay? I wouldn't butt in except that it's really important."

Without pausing to give Pres a chance to interrupt, she repeated the story of Patrick's visit to Haven Lake Medical Center. "It's probably none of our business," she finished, "but we figured you ought to know. I mean, if Claudia needs an operation, you might be a person she cares enough about to listen to."

Pres's expression hadn't changed, but he'd been squeezing the empty can in his hand so hard that it was completely flattened. When Angie stopped talking, he slammed what was left of the can down on the counter so hard that she almost

119

wanted to turn and run out of the store right then.

"I don't believe any of this," he said. "Surely you don't think I'm going to take Patrick Henley's word over Claudia's. This is probably some kind of sick joke he dreamed up."

"Pres, it isn't," Angie promised him. "I know this is hard to listen to, but it's serious."

"Oh come on, Ange. You know Patrick. And Mary Ellen probably put him up to it. She's always liked me, and she just can't stand the thought that I've found someone I like more than her. A hundred times more, for that matter."

"Pres, it isn't that way. You know they wouldn't do that to you," Angie protested. "This is important. And we decided to tell you because we care about you. . . ."

Pres reached out and gave Angie a brotherly pat on the back. "Okay, Ange. I know you aren't part of the plan. But don't you see, Patrick and Mary Ellen put you up to this. I know you can't help being gullible."

"What I'm telling you is the truth, Pres. If you don't want to believe it, fine. But don't call me gullible."

Angie fished some change out of her tote bag, threw it down on the counter, and strode out of the store. Pres watched her go in silence. He couldn't squelch the nagging suspicion that what Angie had said really was the truth. But he couldn't accept it, either. He'd only known Claudia for a short while, but he certainly knew her better than anyone else in Tarenton. She was a terrific girl. If what Angie had said was right, then Claudia had been lying to him ever since the first moment they met. He just wasn't going to believe that.

It was almost a mile from the store to Angie's house, and the walk gave Angie plenty of time to think over Pres's accusation. She was sure that Mary Ellen had been serious. They hadn't been playing a joke on Pres or on her.

On the other hand, she couldn't entirely blame Pres for not listening to her. After all, she'd been naive enough to believe that so-called Reese Oliver when he told her he was a fashion photographer and wanted her to model for him. Good old Angie Poletti, sweet but gullible! That was probably the way everybody in school thought of her. Everybody's buddy, but nobody's girl friend.

All that was going to have to end right now. She'd had enough. She was going to start right away to work on changing her image.

When she got home, her mother was still busy in the beauty salon that she operated from the ground floor of the split-level house. It was her night for late appointments, so she'd probably be working for hours yet. Her brother Andrew was in the kitchen, making himself an omelette.

"I'm going over to Kerry's tonight," he told her. "A bunch of us are getting together to study for a big history test. I've got a ride, so if you want to use the VW, you can."

"As a matter of fact, I do want to use it. Thanks."

"Where are you going?" Andrew asked.

"Oh, no place special. I just need to get out," Angie said.

In fact, she really didn't have any idea where she was going.

In her room, Angie rifled through her closet looking for a change of clothes to suit her mood. Nothing she saw pleased her. She didn't have a huge wardrobe like Nancy's. Nancy, she thought, probably gives away more clothes than I buy. But that wasn't the whole problem. She didn't have Mary Ellen's taste, either. Or Olivia's petite figure, which made her look good no matter what, even in sweats.

Her own closet was less than well-stocked. And what was there ran to preppy plaids and bland neutral colors and saccharine pastels. The styles were all basic and unadventurous. If these clothes could talk, they'd go around announcing: Don't pay any attention to me. I'm nice but dull.

After much deliberation, Angie finally settled on a burgundy-colored blouse and a pair of black slacks. She hadn't worn the slacks in over a year, and she noticed with irritation that they were now just a little bit too tight for her. But at least they weren't boring beige.

In the bathroom, she studied herself in the mirror. At least a new hairstyle didn't cost money. She pulled her honey-blonde hair back off her face and twisted it into a knot at the nape of her neck. That, plus carefully applied eye makeup, made her look years older, she decided. To complete the change she borrowed a pair of large gold hoop earrings from her mother's jewelry box.

122

Not great, she told herself, studying the total effect in the mirror. But at least I don't look like the same old Angie.

The trouble was, where did you go in Tarenton on a Thursday night to try out a new image? There weren't a whole lot of places to go, period.

She drove around for almost an hour before she had an idea. Garry's was a restaurant and roadhouse that had live country music on weekends. It catered mostly to a crowd that liked customized cars and auto racing, but it wasn't so disreputable that she couldn't go in alone to the restaurant part and order a hamburger. At least not early on a weekday evening.

As she pulled into the parking lot, Angie had visions of herself getting into a conversation with a handsome stranger. Maybe a guy from out of town who was out of school for a few years and owned one of those classic cars. Like an old fifties T-bird. Or a huge Buick from the sixties. Mary Ellen would go crazy with envy if she showed up around town with a great-looking guy in a car like that!

At first, the inside of Garry's was disappointing. The restaurant was nearly empty. Angie sat at a small table covered by a red and white checkered cloth and ordered a barbecue roll from a bored-looking waitress. A plaintive country ballad was playing on the jukebox. It made her feel more desperate than ever.

What a dumb plan this was, she told herself. Obviously, this place didn't get lively until late at night and on weekends. Here she was trying to do something daring for once, and she couldn't even get it right!

"Hey there, foxy lady."

The voice belonged to a short, muscular young man who'd been seated alone in a booth across the room. Without waiting for an invitation, he came over and joined Angie at her table.

"My name's Lightning," he said. He turned around to demonstrate a silver lightning bolt that was printed on the back of his black windbreaker jacket.

"It is?"

Angie must have seemed less impressed with the nickname than most girls Lightning met. Her puzzled response made him laugh. "Really, it's Lester Lightner. But I hate my first name, so we'll let it be a secret between the two of us, okay?"

Angie told Lightning her first name. She didn't mention that she was still in high school. It just didn't seem to be the sort of information Lightning expected to hear.

"Can I buy you a drink?" Lightning offered.

"Uh, no thanks," Angie refused.

"Don't worry about being carded," Lightning said. "I know the bartender here. He won't ask any questions."

"No, it's okay, really. I don't drink."

Lightning seemed to find this information startling. As if Angie had just admitted to having some secret deformity or bad habit that a polite person wouldn't mention in public. After that, the conversation lagged.

Angie had been preparing herself to meet someone who'd be excitingly different, even a little dangerous. Lightning was different and slightly scary all right, but at the same time he was boring.

I may not be smart enough to keep up with Arne, but I'm too smart for this guy, Angie told herself.

A slightly sour smell told her that Lightning had been drinking beer. What really bothered her, though, was that Lightning seemed to be sizing her up. And in a way that did not necessarily suggest that he was attracted to her.

Angie pushed her half-eaten sandwich away and began looking around for the waitress. Instinct told her she ought to pay her check and get going.

"Hey, don't run out on me," Lightning said, reading her mind. "We could go for a ride or something. Have a little fun."

"No thanks. I have to be home soon. In fact, they're probably wondering where I am right now," Angie lied.

Lightning grinned, not at all pleasantly. "Okay," he said. "I get the picture. You're not interested. But maybe I do have something you'd be interested in."

He pulled a small jewelry box from his pocket and flipped it open. "You look like a girl who appreciates good jewelry. I could give you a special price. On account of that I like you."

Angie stared at the contents of the small red velvet box. The ring had a very unusual design.

125

The center of the ring was a gold miniature head with two faces, which appeared to be looking in opposite directions. Surrounding the faces was a circle of red and white stones. Angie didn't know anything much about jewelry, but the stones looked real enough.

What interested her more, though, was the design. Two faces, she thought. Two-faced. That certainly fit, since the ring must be stolen, or Lightning wouldn't be trying to sell it to a stranger he'd just met in Garry's. But why would anyone want a ring that symbolized being two-faced?

Uh-uh, she told herself. Probably the design had something to do with twins. . . .

"Gemini!"

She clapped her hand over her mouth, but it was too late. Before she could stop herself, she'd said it out loud.

CHAPTER

 12

Claudia's deep violet eyes were teary with emotion. She pulled away from Pres's kiss and snuggled down into the curve of his arm. "I have a confession to make to you," she said.

Pres felt himself choking up inside. All evening he'd been trying to convince himself that Angie's warning was some sort of cruel joke. He'd done a pretty good job of it, too, even though his rational mind knew better. Now Claudia was going to spoil everything.

"I'm not really a nursing student," Claudia said. "I'm really just staying with the Harroldsons as a house guest."

"I know," Pres said, his voice drained of emotion.

"You do?" Claudia pretended to be delighted that the truth was out in the open. "Then why didn't you say so? Why did you just go on letting me make a little fool out of myself?"

"It seems to me," said Pres, "that I'm the one who should be asking that question."

"But I never actually said I was studying nursing," Claudia protested. "Not in so many words, anyway. You jumped to that conclusion, and I was afraid to tell you the truth. I thought you'd think more of me if I told you I was a student."

"Claudia, I couldn't think any more of you than I already do. I'm crazy about you. But I wish you'd been honest with me."

"Okay," said Claudia.

Pres thought uneasily that Claudia was agreeing too quickly, as if he had just suggested a new game for them to play. But honesty was definitely not a game.

"The truth is," said Claudia, "I'm just staying with the Harroldsons as a house guest. I couldn't be a nursing student because I never even finished my senior year in high school. Personally, I don't mind being a dropout. School was boring. A waste of time. But I figured you might not see it that way."

"And that's all?" asked Pres, incredulous.

"Why, Pres, I don't know what you're talking about!" Claudia purred back. "Of course, that's all."

They had been sitting in the big leather couch in the Tilford den. Suddenly the room, with its cozy fire burning in the fireplace and its dim, romantic lighting, no longer seemed quite so idyllic. Claudia had no intention of leveling with him. She was just switching from one lie to another.

Pres pulled away from her and stood up.

"That's not the story I heard," he said. Briefly, he started to repeat what Patrick had overheard at the hospital.

"Your friends have been spying on me!" she broke in, before the story was half finished. "Besides, it isn't so. You have no right to believe them."

Pres felt as if he was being torn in two. What he wanted to do was take Claudia in his arms and hold her, so that they could comfort each other. Instead he was locked into this stupid argument. And all because Claudia didn't trust him enough to tell the truth. That part of it hurt badly.

"If it isn't true," Pres said, "then prove it. Go skiing with me."

Claudia's face turned ashy white. "I don't know how to ski," she protested.

"I'll teach you," Pres said. "Live for today, isn't that your motto? Make the most of every minute. How can you pass up a chance to learn to ski?"

Claudia's eyes filled with tears of anger. "Have it your way. It is true. Do you want the clinical details? I have a bone chip lodged near my spine and physical activity might cause it to shift and injure my spinal cord. In fact, the doctors say that will probably happen eventually anyway. When it does, I'll be paralyzed for life.

"Now you know," she added defiantly, "so you

can start pitying me like everyone else."

"It isn't pity I feel," Pres contradicted her. "I care about you."

"Oh sure," said Claudia skeptically. "You're the one who told me how sick people gave you the creeps, remember? You couldn't understand how anyone would even want to go into nursing. Are you trying to tell me that if you'd known about my problem from the beginning you wouldn't have treated me in a completely different way?"

She has me there, Pres thought. He wanted to deny it. But it was true that if he'd known what Claudia was facing, he never would have let himself fall in love with her. At the very least he wouldn't have fallen as hard and fast as he did. He would have kept his distance emotionally.

"Maybe you're partly right," he admitted out loud. "I'm sorry about that. But right now, all I want is what's best for you. I can't understand why you won't have that operation."

"Because I'm scared, that's why," she told him. "Because I'm even more scared of dying on the operating table than I am of being paralyzed."

Pres sat back down and put his arms around her. "Oh, Claudia, I'm so sorry," he said. "It scares me, too. But you can't just give up. Somehow you've got to get over being scared. The doctors wouldn't want you to have that operation if it weren't the best thing for you."

She pushed him away. "That, Pres Tilford, is what everyone tells me. But you don't know what it's like to be me, and neither does anyone else. You have no right to give me advice."

"Oh yes, I do," Pres said. "I love you. That gives me the right."

Claudia laughed. The sound, which had once made Pres's heart skip a beat with joy, now sounded hollow and incongruous. "You're not in love with me," she told him. "You're in love with happy-go-lucky Claudia, the 'live for today' girl. You don't even know the real Claudia Randall.

"Besides," she added, "how can you lecture me on being brave when you've never had to face a problem like mine? You've never had a worry in your entire life more serious than wondering which girl you're going to chase next, or maybe plotting to escape from your parents' plans to make you a rich businessman. Those aren't real problems. I know, believe me, because my life used to be the same way before this stupid accident."

After that, there didn't seem to be much left to say.

Pres helped Claudia into her coat, and they got into his car for the drive back to the Harroldsons'. Sitting in the driver's seat of his red Porsche with a silent, withdrawn Claudia beside him, Pres tried to figure out how it was possible for a dream to go sour so quickly. He'd thought that he and Claudia had experienced love at first sight. Now she was telling him that the girl he cared for didn't even exist.

When they got to the Harroldsons', Pres tried one more time. "I didn't mean to hurt you,

Claudia," he began. "If you don't want to talk about it, fine. We'll go back to the way we were."

"It can't ever be like that again," Claudia said bitterly. "It's all ruined." And she sprang out of the car and left before Pres could say any more.

What could I have said, anyway? Pres asked himself as he swung a U-ey in the Harroldsons' driveway. Claudia was right. Everything was ruined. And it was going to be a long, lonely drive back to Tarenton.

Inside Garry's, meanwhile, Angie was grinning. A big flirtatious grin that she felt sure must be the least convincing come-on look in history.

Lightning was studying her face, his eyes percolating with suspicion and calculation.

I know where that ring came from. And he knows I know, thought Angie.

Fortunately, despite his name, Lightning was not a fast thinker. It was going to take him a while to figure out what to do about Angie. She decided that she'd better have her plans made before then.

She forced herself to smile. "It's a really *great* ring, you know," she gulped. "But that isn't my sign. Anyway, I'm broke right now. I can barely put gas in the car."

Lightning looked momentarily confused.

"Actually, maybe I do know someone who'd be interested in that ring," Angie lied.

"Oh yeah, who?"

Chief Danielli, Angie wanted to say, but she bit her tongue in time. She knew she had to come up with a name, but her mind was completely blank. "Uh, her name's Vanessa," she blurted out finally. "Vanessa Barlow. She's in the phone book."

"Okay, so call her," Lightning said. "Tell her to come over here."

"Uh, now?"

"Now."

He wants to sell the ring to someone I know, Angie figured. That way I'll be guilty, too, and he won't have to worry about me turning him in.

"Okay," she said, smiling weakly. "I'll go call her."

Fortunately, the phone booths were by the main door, just out of sight of their table. As she was heading their way, Angie fumbled in her purse for a bill large enough to cover her check and plunked it down by the cash register. She didn't even bother to glance at the phone booths but sprinted for the door. No sense giving Lightning a chance to figure out that he was being too trusting.

Lightning's jeep was parked just outside. It had to be his, because he'd customized it with painted silver lightning blots on the front and rear fenders. Angie could see that at a glance it would be easy to mistake the decorations for the silver tape that was on Walt's jeep.

She didn't stop to think about this too long, though. As quickly as possible, she got into the VW, turned the key in the ignition, and got the car in gear.

Everything was going fine until she tried to

133

shift in reverse and the engine gave a sickly cough and died on her.

Andrew had warned her that the transmission could be tricky. You have to let the car warm up first, Angie reminded herself. Be patient. But at the moment she didn't have time to be patient. Her second try was no more successful than her first. And by the third try she was wondering if she'd managed to flood the carburetor.

Angie reminded herself that Lightning had no idea what her car looked like. He was going to be coming out to look for her any second. The thing to do was to get out of the car and hide somewhere. He'd assume she already left, and then when he was gone she could come back and take her time starting the car.

Moving fast, she slipped out of the driver's seat and started to make her way down toward the end of the parking lot. There were a couple of vans down there that she could hide behind.

"Hey, come back here! You tricked me!" She heard Lightning's voice shouting from the direction of the door.

Angie broke into a run. Now she'd really outsmarted herself. She'd been seen.

Looking back over her shoulder, Angie saw that Lightning had no intention of getting into a foot race. As soon as she broke in the direction of the road, he'd headed for his jeep. It wasn't even going to be a fair contest.

Angie waved her arms frantically. She could never get past Lightning and make it back to the front door of Garry's. Flagging down a car on the road was her only chance. The first four cars sped past without stopping. Then, just when she was almost ready to give up, the fifth came to a screeching halt at her side. She would have recognized Pres Tilford's red Porsche anywhere, but she never thought she'd be this glad to see it.

"Pres! Is that really you?" she said, fighting for breath. "Someone's chasing me."

"Then get in. Don't just stand there."

Angie scrambled into the passenger seat, and Pres stepped on the gas. The headlights of Lightning's jeep followed them for a mile or so, then disappeared.

"He's given up," Pres said. "Don't worry, everything's all right."

Hurriedly, Angie explained what had happened. She didn't go into details about what she was doing at Garry's in the first place, and he was too tactful to ask.

"Andrew's car is back there," she wailed. "Now what am I going to do? He'll kill me."

"Don't worry," Pres reassured her. "Somehow I don't think Lightning is going to be heading back to Garry's. Walt's house is pretty near here. We'll stop there and you can call the police and tell them what happened. Walt and I can go back later and get your car."

The Mannerses' house was located on a stretch of country road that was usually deserted after dark. Tonight, however, Pres and Angie found themselves creeping along behind an old car that was moving down the two-lane highway at a snail's pace. To their surprise, the car flashed its signals just as it approached Walt's house and turned ahead of them into the Mannerses' driveway.

"Looks like we're not Walt's only visitor tonight," Angie said as Olivia got out of the other car and headed for the front door. "It must be important. Olivia never drives her parents' car if she can help it."

Olivia looked completely surprised to see that she'd arrived at the same time as Pres and Angie. They were just as surprised to see her. While they were all standing around trying to figure out what to say, Walt opened the door.

"What's this?" he asked suspiciously. "Some kind of delegation?"

Olivia was the first to find her tongue. "I came by myself," she announced. "If you don't want to talk to me, fine. But I have something to say to your folks."

"My folks?"

"I heard what they said on their show, and it made me mad," Olivia explained. "They never talk about the good things you do. They never talk about your being a cheerleader and things like that. The only time they mention your name is when you get in trouble.

"I thought someone should tell them that," she finished more hesitantly. "You know, sometimes parents don't think. . . ."

Walt could hardly believe it. No one in his whole life had understood how he sometimes felt about having his life turned into material for his parents' TV show. No one except Olivia. He knew that it took a lot of courage for her to even think of talking to them about it, too. Olivia had always acted shy and practically speechless around his parents.

"Livvy, that's great. You're wonderful," Walt said, sweeping her up in a big hug.

Pres cleared his throat. "Excuse us," he said. "We don't mean to interrupt the course of true love. But the reason we're here, which you don't seem in any hurry to ask about, is because we need to call the police."

That was good enough to get Walt and Olivia's attention for at least a few minutes. Pres and Angie took turns explaining about Lightning and the stolen ring. Then, while Olivia went off to have her heart-to-heart talk with Walt's parents, the others went into the kitchen to call Chief Danielli.

"It looks like my luck has really changed," Walt said after they'd finished on the phone. "Chief Danielli says he and the State Patrol will be looking out for this Lightning character. They're sure to pick him up pretty soon. And Olivia isn't mad at me anymore. Isn't it great what teamwork will do? See? Everything's working out."

Angie sneaked a glance at Pres. As long as the excitement of the chase and getting to Walt's was going on, he'd seemed perfectly fine. Now he seemed to be sinking deeper into gloom by the minute.

She was eager to ask if he'd talked to Claudia. Did he still think that she and Mary Ellen and Patrick had made all that up? But she didn't dare put her questions into words.

CHAPTER

"Don't tell me that you and Ben have made up, too!" Mary Ellen said to Nancy.

It was a dumb question in a way, because she'd timed Nancy's good-bye kiss to Ben at a minute and a half. And Ben wasn't even going anywhere — just down to the varsity locker room to change for tonight's game.

Nancy tried to look guilty but her brown eyes were glowing with happiness. "I guess we've worked things out. I was dumb to walk out on Ben at the pool party and try to make him jealous. And he was dumb to do the same thing to me. We figured we were even, so we might as well make up."

Mary Ellen blinked. That was a new one on her. Two jealousies canceling each other out. Or two dumb mistakes, for that matter. If that were true, she and Patrick ought to be getting along fine.

"Do you mean that you think it will really work out between the two of you now?"

Nancy shrugged. "Who knows? I'm not sure Ben and I are right for each other. But I like him enough to try. If you don't take chances, you never win the prize.

"I hear Walt and Olivia are an item again, too," Nancy was saying.

"That's right," Mary Ellen told her. "But I'm afraid we've got another slight problem. Dr. Barlow called me and Walt in early for a little pregame conference in Coach Engborg's office. He's on the warpath again."

"But why?" Nancy, her own problems solved, considered the troubles of the past week over and done with. She was surprised to hear that Dr. Barlow was still all worked up.

"He said he doesn't want to see the squad or any of its members getting any more bad publicity," Mary Ellen explained. "Bad for the school image, and all that. You should have heard him."

"But that's unfair!" Nancy protested.

"Sure it's unfair. Coach is on our side. And he was a little bit mollified when he heard that Walt's parents are going to give the cheerleading squad a nice plug on one of their shows. But I'll still be relieved when the police finally catch that Lightning guy. It's two days now and no one's seen him."

"Don't worry," Nancy advised. "And forget Dr. Barlow. He's all bark and no bite."

That was easy for Nancy to say, Mary Ellen thought. Nancy wasn't intimidated by Dr. Barlow, even if he was superintendent of schools. Because her parents had clout. And they'd take her side no matter what.

She tried to shake off the thought and get back into the right spirit for tonight's game. It wasn't Dr. Barlow that was bothering her anyway. It was envy. Envy at seeing Nancy and Ben, and Olivia and Walt, too, back together again.

Even Pres had taken a chance and let himself fall in love with Claudia. If it was true about Claudia's problems, then you couldn't exactly envy either her or Pres. But at least they had each other. At least they'd had happy times together.

She and Patrick had been going around in circles long before either of those couples got together. And they weren't any farther along toward working things out than they'd ever been.

Maybe Nancy was right. You had to be willing to take a chance. Other people just plunged right in. Fell in love and then did their best to work things out. But she, Mary Ellen Kirkwood, couldn't do that — because she had to know how everything was going to work out before she even let herself get past square one.

The spectator seats were filling rapidly. Tonight's game was against Grove Lake, and it was a must for Tarenton's chances of a conference title.

Mary Ellen took her place in the hall outside the gym and waited for the other members of

141

the squad to join her. When they were all ready, Ardith gave the signal and they made their entrance — leapfrogging their way down the aisle and then spreading out in front of the home team seats to lead the crowd in the fight cheer.

Megaphone in hand, Mary Ellen called out the letters as the others on the squad took turns forming them in groups of two and three:

"Give me a T. . . . Give me an A. . . ."

By the time they reached the end of the cheer, Mary Ellen's enthusiasm was genuine. "Whadda ya got?" she exulted, shouting loud enough to be heard all the way to Grove Lake.

"TARENTON!!!" the crowd roared.

She leaped into the air, her back arched and her red and white cheerleader's skirt swirling around her. No matter how crazy life got, cheering always made her feel good.

Angie, jumping up and down in celebration of an early Tarenton score, was thinking much the same thing.

Olivia and Nancy had forgotten their differences, and as soon as the first time out was called, they ran arm in arm across the court, ready to drum up a little enthusiasm from the adult spectators in the reserved seats.

Even Walt seemed to have forgotten that Ben Adamson was not exactly his favorite person. It was a close, fast-paced game, and every time Ben picked up a rebound Walt cheered as loudly as anyone else.

"Team spirit conquers all," Mary Ellen said out loud happily.

The only member of the squad who was not cheering with all his heart was Pres Tilford. But from the outside, who could tell? Blond, all-American Pres had the looks that the rest of the world associated with being carefree and upbeat.

No one expected Preston Tilford III to have a heart that could be broken.

Pres felt that he was dying inside. He couldn't believe that it wasn't obvious to every single person in the stands. Yet somehow it wasn't. Just before the game Coach Engborg had asked, with mild concern, if he had an upset stomach. And Angie kept giving him funny looks.

But that was it. Mary Ellen didn't even seem to realize that Angie had gotten around to talking to him about Claudia.

Pres stuffed his private sorrow a little farther down inside himself and concentrated on going through the motions of the cheering routines. From now on he was going to play it cool. Having feelings was just too risky.

In the fourth quarter the game was still so close that the lead changed sides three times.

Completely caught up in the game, Mary Ellen kept the squad working hard, pumping up the crowd to a fever pitch. With five seconds left on the clock, Tarenton was ahead by two, but Grove Lake had possession and was driving for another score.

Suddenly Ben Adamson — lanky, hawklike

Ben — seemed to swoop out of nowhere and picked off the ball in midpass. Everyone held their breath as Ben loped back downcourt on a fast break and lobbed the ball into the basket.

The buzzer sounded almost simultaneously. And the home crowd went wild with delight. The final score was Tarenton, 76, Grove Lake, 72.

By the time the excitement had settled down, the visiting cheerleaders had already left the court.

"Come on, guys," Mary Ellen said. "Let's go out into the hall and wait for them. We can shake hands with them and the Grove Lake team, too! Good sportsmanship, forever. And especially when we've won."

She led the way through the departing crowds and through the gym doors — and walked right into a phalanx of microphones.

Just as Walt and Nancy had been the previous week, Mary Ellen was momentarily stunned. It occurred to her first that this must have something to do with the Mannerses' plan to do a segment on cheerleading. But they'd never said they were actually going to do any filming. The Mannerses hardly ever used film clips like that. Mostly they sat around the breakfast table and gave their opinions on what was wrong with the world.

Then she noticed that the camera team was from Channel Eight. Her heart sank. "What's going on. . . ?" she started to say.

A strong, protective hand reached out of the crowd and grabbed Mary Ellen's arm, pulling her out of the range of the microphones.

144

She knew it was Patrick even before she turned around. "Don't worry," he said quickly. "They don't want you. Just watch."

At that moment, Dr. Barlow bustled out into the hall and headed for the film crew. He was in his attack mode.

"You don't have permission to be here," he complained. "What's this all about?"

The young woman reporter looked unimpressed. Mary Ellen noticed that the cameras were running.

"And who might you be?" the reporter asked.

"I am Dr. Fredrick Barlow," Dr. Barlow said, as if for anyone not to know this was the epitome of ignorance.

"Is your daughter Vanessa Barlow?"

"Yes, of course. . . ."

The reporter moved the microphone in closer under Dr. Barlow's chin. "And what's your reaction to your daughter being arrested for possession of stolen property?"

"What? That's not true!" Dr. Barlow sputtered. "Even Vanessa wouldn't be that stupid. I mean, she doesn't have to buy stolen property. She's already got closetsful of things. What I mean is, I'm sure there must be some mistake."

"Oh, there's no mistake," the reporter said. "Your daughter *says* she agreed to buy the goods only because she was conducting an independent investigation of the theft on your behalf."

Dr. Barlow's face turned the color of a boiled beet. "She said *that*?" he exploded. "Why, I'll wring her neck.

145

"I mean, I won't really," he said, remembering who he was talking to. "But it isn't so. I assure you. And furthermore, no comment."

"And that," laughed Walt, who'd been watching Dr. Barlow with interest, "is a lesson from our superintendent of schools on how to deal with the media."

"For once," said Mary Ellen, "I have to agree with Dr. Barlow, though. I mean the part about Vanessa not being quite crazy enough to buy stolen property. Why would she do a thing like that?"

"It's true, though," said Patrick. "She'd made an appointment to meet this Lightning character down the road from the school just before the game. Fortunately for Vanessa, Sergeant Danielli knows she isn't fencing stolen property. I'm sure he isn't serious about pressing charges. He'll let her off if she agrees to make a statement against Lightning."

"Figure it out," Nancy put in. "As long as Vanessa had the evidence, the case would never be closed. I wouldn't be surprised if she was going to plant that ring on Walt. Or even on me. I'm the Gemini, remember."

"That's the why," said Walt. "What I don't get is the how. Even the police couldn't find this guy Lightning. How did Vanessa find him?"

Angie had been listening in silence. She could feel her ears turning hot from embarrassment. She was probably starting to blush, which she always hated. "I've got an awful confession to make," she said. "I sicked Lightning on Vanessa.

146

But I didn't mean to! Her name just popped into my head!"

Patrick roared with laughter. Then, one by one, the others broke up, too.

"Anyone else could have plotted for weeks and still never have figured out a way to set Vanessa up like that," Nancy said. "But you just seem to have the knack. You luck into these incredible adventures."

"I do?" Angie blinked. This was a view of herself she'd never considered before.

"Sure, that's why we all love you, Angie," Patrick said.

"You do?" Angie asked in astonishment.

"Of course we do," Walt chimed in. He gave Angie a big hug. Then Olivia joined in. Then Nancy, and Patrick and Mary Ellen.

But not even Dr. Barlow's little press conference had been able to distract Pres Tilford from his depression. He'd wandered off in the middle of all the excitement, his mind still churning over the words of one of the last cheers of the evening: "Got the spirit. Let's hear it."

Well, he *didn't* have the spirit. And no one was going to hear about it.

Pres made his way back into the gym and stood surveying the empty rows of bleachers. Why hadn't he ever noticed before that basketball was a stupid, meaningless game?

"Great game, wasn't it?" said a voice behind him.

Pres turned around and found himself looking

147

into the face he loved. Claudia's face.

"What are you doing here?" he gasped.

"I hope you don't mind," Claudia said. "I wanted to see you cheer before I left. You never told me you were really good."

"I'm glad you came," Pres said.

Then gradually, Claudia's words started to sink in. "Before you leave?" he asked. "Does that mean you're going back home to Virginia?"

Claudia shook her head. "No. To California. There's this operation I need to have. Remember?"

"You changed your mind? Oh, Claudia, that's great!"

"I didn't change my mind. You changed it," she said.

"But I thought you were mad at me for even trying to talk about it."

"It isn't what you said," Claudia explained. "It was just you. Your being there. I'd convinced myself that if I couldn't face going through with that operation, it was my problem. So what if I ended up in a wheelchair sooner or later? No one would be hurt but me.

"You," she went on, "made me realize that isn't so. I have to think about other people, too. And in the meantime, I couldn't even talk to you. I had to pretend to be a different kind of person completely. All because I didn't want you to know that the real Claudia was a coward."

"I'd never think you were a coward. . . ."

Claudia laughed. That soft, silky laugh that

was like no other laugh Pres had ever heard. "That's not what you said the other day. Besides, it will work out. Dr. Harroldson says my chances are ninety percent."

"Ninety percent?" All the time Pres had been trying to convince Claudia to have the operation, the reality of what might happen if it didn't work out hadn't quite sunk in. "Translated, does that mean there's a one in ten chance that you'll die?"

"Not necessarily. It could just mean I'll end up paralyzed anyway. Only sooner."

Claudia looked up at him. "Please, Pres. I've made up my mind. Don't get me scared all over again."

"Okay."

"Are you coming back here when it's over?" he asked.

"I'd love to. But I don't think I can," Claudia said. "I've got to think about finishing high school, for one thing. And then I have to figure out what I want to do next. That's the catch about 'living for today,'" she laughed again. "Once you stop, it seems like you've got a lot of catching up to do."

"Claudia, you've got to come back. I don't want to lose you."

She shook her head. "Please don't get into this, Pres. Not right now. And no big good-byes, either. I just don't think I could stand it. If we start talking about those things now, I'll never have the courage to go."

Before Pres could answer, she turned and walked through the swinging doors that led out into the hall.

Pres didn't try to stop her. Claudia had come into his life unexpectedly and turned all his feelings upside down. And now she was gone. It was almost as if he'd imagined the whole thing.

But, at least, for her, the dream might have a happy ending. He hoped so. He hoped he'd helped her to make the right decision. That was the part he didn't like to think too much about. Because the stakes for Claudia were so high.

Pres picked up a basketball and started dribbling it thoughtfully across the court.

Outside in the hall, someone threw a switch, turning off the ceiling lights and plunging the gym into semidarkness. The eerie glow of the red safety lights above the exit doors was just enough to let Pres get a good bead on the basket. He launched a one-handed shot and watched it sink through the hoop.

Maybe basketball wasn't so bad after all, he thought. At least you knew the rules. Knew what you had to do to win. Life was a lot riskier. And a lot more confusing.

Outside in the parking lot, Mary Ellen was getting into Patrick Henley's truck. She'd changed into her street clothes and they were heading off to an impromptu party that Nancy was giving to celebrate getting back together with Ben.

"You look terrific," Patrick said appreciatively. "I hate to seem suspicious," he added, "but how come you asked me to take you to this party? I mean, we're actually having a real date, and I didn't have to trick you into it."

"I'd sort of decided earlier," Mary Ellen said mysteriously.

"But then," she added, "I ran into Claudia in the hall. Pres's girl. She told me she'd decided to have that operation after all."

"That's a relief. But what's the connection?"

"Well, I figured that if she has the courage to face all that, I shouldn't be scared of my feelings for you."

"Great," he said. "A date with Patrick Henley ranks only slightly higher than a serious operation on your scale of horrible ordeals."

"I didn't mean it that way," Mary Ellen said.

It was a brilliantly clear night, and there were so many stars overhead that they seemed to be almost crowding each other for room to shine. In her mind, all the dreams she had for her future were just as jumbled up. A modeling career. Travel. Success. Money. And Patrick. The possibility that maybe she couldn't have them all, that she would eventually have to take a chance on committing herself to one goal, was scary. Even if she couldn't quite explain that to Patrick.

"Let's not talk about it tonight," she said. "Let's just go over to Nancy's and try to enjoy ourselves for once, without getting into some kind of argument."

"That's fine with me," Patrick said.

He'd noticed that Mary Ellen had taken her hair out of the little braids she'd worn during the game and let it fall loose, framing her face. Her hair looked so incredibly soft and silky. Like cornsilk.

He wanted to tell her that, but he didn't quite dare. For all he knew, Mary Ellen didn't think cornsilk was beautiful. He was afraid she'd laugh at him for thinking of such a dumb comparison.

Instead, he reached out with his big, work-hardened palm and stroked her hair, ever so lightly. "I really am crazy about you, Mary Ellen," he said, "even if I don't always understand you."

"That's okay," she told him. "For right now anyway, maybe that's enough."

Patrick leaned over and kissed her deeply, then turned his attention to getting the truck started. They pulled out of the parking lot and rode on in silence, Patrick humming contentedly and Mary Ellen watching the yellow line of the road unfurl in front of her. It was true. For right now she felt that glow of happiness that she always felt when she heard the sound of Patrick's deep, baritone voice singing for her. She only wished she knew for sure where this road was going to take her.

Will New York City steal Mary Ellen's heart from Patrick? Read Cheerleaders #14, LIVING IT UP.

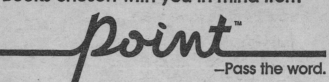